MURDERGIRL

IN THE VALLEY OF THE BONES

JONATHAN-DAVID
JACKSON

Murdergirl in the Valley of the Bones
(Murdergirl: Book One)

Written by
Jonathan-David Jackson

ISBN 978-1-915923-54-7

Cover Illustration by
Marc Bonavia (mbonav96.artstation.com)

Cover Design by
Jonathan-David Jackson

Published by
Affordable Classics Ltd

Other books by Jonathan-David Jackson

Dark Humor Trilogy
The Quest for Juice
The Quest for Truth
The Quest for Nothing in Particular

Supernatural Thriller
Faith of the Forsaken

Gentle Postapocalyptic Dark Humor
Not Quite the End of the World

For my brother,
Michael-Andrew.

If I had to be in a post-apocalyptic wasteland, I'd want you there too.

Chapter 1

Murdergirl looked down at the teenage girl. The male baby the girl held was thin, ribs showing as he sucked desperately at her dry breast. Her red hair laid over his back. Murdergirl tugged on the end of her own dark ponytail which came halfway down her chest and glanced around. The rest of the Bones were already moving on. She grabbed a sack from the back of the cart before it got away. No idea what was in it, but it would at least be food. The old woman sitting near the girl started to thank her, but Murdergirl brought her finger up to her lips. The woman's eyes thanked her, and she smiled in return. Then she turned to join the others before they noticed.

A man a head taller than her, with a hat two heads taller still, stepped in front of her. "Where are you going in such a hurry?"

"I'm taking my place by the cart, Hambone."

He smiled, with impossibly white teeth made whiter by the dark skin of his face. "There's no rush. Let's stop and visit for a while with Rebecca."

"But the cart—"

He gripped her shoulder. "The cart will wait."

"Hambone," Rebecca said as a greeting.

Hambone removed his top hat and bowed to the old woman. Murdergirl looked everywhere; the Gardeners had hidden the bag of food well.

"I see there's a new baby in the Garden," Hambone said.

"Yes," Rebecca replied.

"Good, good." He smiled. "Children are our future, are they not?" He bent down and tipped up the chin of the girl. "And you, young one? Is this your baby?" The girl, with lips pressed tight together, shook her head. "All women should experience the joy of motherhood," he said. "But you're young. There is time."

He straightened up. "Now, Rebecca..." He swooped down and snatched the baby from the girl's breast, "... what is our arrangement?"

"Hambone, please!" Rebecca sprang to her feet, faster than Murdergirl had thought the old woman could move.

The girl leapt up and reached for the baby, but Hambone held it high. "Sit down," he commanded, over the cries of the baby. The girl stood, fists clenched at her hips, jaw set. The white skin of her face and chest had turned pink.

"Harissa," Rebecca said. She put her hand on the girl's shoulder. They made eye contact, and with a great exhalation of breath through her nose, Harissa sat.

"Very good," Hambone said. He lowered the child and cradled it against his own body with one arm. "What is our agreement, Rebecca?"

"We make the food, and the Bones take the food."

He laughed. "Very good, yes. And in return, we provide protection."

She pointed a finger at the baby. "Is this protection?"

"The child is not harmed, is it? And we have not harmed you, yet you have taken food out of our mouths."

Murdergirl gritted her teeth. *Fuck.*

Hambone gripped the baby by the neck and held it in front of his face. "Like this infant, you need constant care and protection."

"It's just before the harvest. You haven't left us enough—"

"And without that protection, where would the infant be?" He tossed the baby on the ground. Harissa jumped up, but Hambone lifted his boot and shoved her back down before she could get on her feet. The baby cried weakly and waved its arms and legs, sand coating its skin as it wriggled. Murdergirl moved to pick it up herself, but by now more Bones had joined them, and Davey stepped in front of her to block her path.

"Just like you would be, the infant is now lost and helpless, at the mercy of anyone who wishes it harm. Our agreement is what holds society together."

"Do you really call this society?" Rebecca asked. "In the times before—"

"Those times are gone. Now, the weak serve the strong." He picked up the baby, took a flask from his hip, and poured water over it to clean the sand away. "And the strong protect the weak."

He handed the baby to Harissa, who sat with eyes blazing and tears on her cheeks.

"Let's go!" Hambone shouted, and circled his hand above his head. Murdergirl took her place beside the cart and they left the village.

She trudged beside the long, eight-wheeled cart, pushing against the bar which propelled the cart forward. On each side, at every set of wheels, a pair of men from the gang pushed. In front, half a dozen pulled it with harnesses. The rest of the gang walked at a distance—*outriders*, a word from when people didn't walk everywhere. She walked at the rear, with Murderboy on the opposite side. The cart was piled high with bamboo cartons and rough sacks. Two women sat in the middle of it all, tied together by their ankles, laughing as they talked with each other. They weren't prisoners, not exactly.

Like every day, the sun shone relentlessly. It warmed the sandy, taupe skin of her hands and soothed the muscles of her arms beneath the light shirt that came to her wrists.

They passed a rusted metal hulk, ten times larger than the cart. A ship, they used to be called. When people talked, they told impossible stories, they said that the water used to be taller than your head, so tall it could cover you completely, and real people lived in the ships under the water. Now, they were only good as a home for spiders and crevice crickets, like most of the things from before.

"How's it going?" Murderboy asked, across the width of cart that separated them. She looked at him without answering, and then turned her eyes forward again. "Come on," he persisted. "It's a long walk back without talking."

She sighed. They had already been walking for over an hour. "It's a long walk either way." And, she didn't say, sometimes it was even longer if he was talking.

"How come you gave the old woman food?"

She didn't answer at first. They were passing the Tomb Tree—a tree older than any of them, dead, with limbs shaped like a cross, that symbol of death that people in the time before had used to mark where they buried a person. "It was for the baby," she said at last.

"But you know the order of things. The strong protect the weak—"

"And the weak serve the strong," she finished. "I know."

"Then why? The baby will live if it should, if it's strong enough."

She looked at him. His shirt sleeves were rolled up nearly to the vest, and sweat shone on the muscles of his arms. He was stronger than her, but not as strong as most of the other Bones.

"Why?" she asked back. "I'm stronger than that old woman, but that's not her fault."

Murderboy shook his head. "It's not about fault. When the desert cat tears out the throat of the badger, nobody is at fault. It's the way things are. When you get your first kill, get your name back, and become a full Bone, you won't be thinking things like this."

It wasn't *right*, but it was true. In every animal, including humans, this was the way things had to be. For as long as they could, she and her mother had tried to live a better way. And without her mother, she'd tried a little bit more on her own until it was impossible. Her life had been more than twenty years, and she still had trouble accepting the way things were.

Chapter 2

Murdergirl sat on an upturned crate in the central area of the Bones' camp. Thick burlap hung from wooden frames to create an area as wide as six people laid head-to-toes. Most other parts of the camp were covered on top, but here it was open to the night sky. Several barrels blazed with flame, roasting some of the food they'd collected from the Garden. Hundreds of books lay piled in a corner. The people before had made enough books to last perhaps until the end of time, and the Bones took advantage of that by collecting them whenever they could be found—they were great for cooking fuel. Every now and then, someone would take a book or two and toss them into a barrel, sending a shower of sparks up to the darkness. Over the flames there was corn—roasted with the husk on—cactus nuts, and sweet potatoes. Her stomach rumbled as she watched the food cook. It would be a good meal, well-earned at the end of a long day.

Behind one of the burlap walls, she heard the laughter of women, the ones who had been tied together on the cart. They weren't Bones—she was the only woman member. They came to the camp, did what the Bones wanted, and in return they would leave with bellies full of food plus as much as they could carry. It was as close to voluntary as anything could be. Nobody forced them to come—the rope around their ankles on the cart was just a formality to stop them backing out of the agreement once made. They were hungry, and they got fed without having to grow food or steal food. It wasn't a bad deal. She'd almost been one of them until Hambone suggested she be their Murdergirl instead. Six months now she'd been without her own name, six months waiting on a kill. There had been a few opportunities, but one of the other Bones had always done it faster. She wanted to move on, to move up. Next time, she wouldn't hesitate.

The laughter had stopped, replaced with moans muffled by full mouths, and quiet cries of pleasure. Real or fake, it didn't matter, though there was a good chance it was real. You had to take pleasure where you could find it, even if it came from a man who was paying you with potatoes and cactus nuts. She felt her breath quickening. Everybody had needs. How long since she'd been underneath a man? Three years? More?

"Come on, I don't want to," she heard one of the women say, and she shook her head. They'd known what they were getting into, it was too late to say no now. She put them out of her head, tried to think of other things. She thought of what was beyond the camp, what was out there. Not much. The Forge and the Garden, the only places worth thinking about. The Oasis, too, if you liked dead trees. Sand, and dry, cracked earth as far as you could see, all the way to the mountains. Maybe somewhere, after weeks of walking, maybe there would be places filled with green plants and wide rivers of running water. She knew there wasn't, but it was nice to think there might be.

The sound of a smack and a scream brought her back to the camp. Then, from behind the burlap wall, quiet weeping. Murdergirl drummed her fingers on her legs and suddenly stood up. She strode to the wall and pulled it aside. The two women, completely naked, and the three men—Davey, Tobas, and another—in various stages of undress, looked at her. One of the women, crouched on the ground and with tears in her eyes, looked away. "You heard her," Murdergirl said. "She doesn't want to do it."

Davey, standing over the crouching woman, said, "Murdergirl, get the fuck out." When she did not get the fuck out, he turned to face her and pulled up his pants as he did, which did not do much to hide the swelling at his crotch. "They both already agreed to it when they agreed to come here. She's eaten." He pointed to several sacks in the corner of the room. "Their supplies are ready for them to take back."

"Let them go." She turned to the crouching woman. "Get your clothes. Go." The woman slowly began to stand up.

"Get the fuck back down," Tobas said, and the woman did, keeping her face lowered. Tobas put his hand on the woman's shoulder. He was naked to his waist, his reddish pubic hair sprouting over the waistband of his pants.

Davey closed his eyes and sighed. "Murdergirl, what is this about? Are you upset because there's no man for you? You're the only woman here. You know we can't go to the effort just for you." He looked down at the woman crouched submissively beside him. "Or is it that you want a turn with them?" He raised an eyebrow and gestured towards the other woman. "Everyone is welcome."

Without really thinking, she snatched up Davey's zip-pistol and pointed it at him. "Whoa, whoa," he said, backing away with his hands up.

Would killing a fellow Bone count as her first? Probably not. If he would just let the women go, it wouldn't even need to come to that. But with the gun, she had the power.

Murderboy was right. There was no fault. It was only power.

Then Davey put his hands down and smirked. "Six months without a kill. I told Hambone when he let you in that you couldn't do it. He said you could." He stepped towards her. "Well, now we see who was right."

She tried to squeeze the trigger, but Davey was right. She couldn't do it. This wasn't something you could kill someone for, when they were just following the natural way of things. And yet, somehow it was all wrong. She pulled the gun close to her, holding the barrel in one hand and the grip in the other. Davey reached out his hand for it. "Hand it over."

She swung the gun, hard, and smashed it into the side of his head. He dropped like a sack of cactus nuts. The two other men looked at each other. "You want the gun, too?" she asked. "Get your things," she said to the women. "Get dressed. Get your food and go."

Unsure, the women gathered their clothes slowly. They looked at the other men, who looked at each other again and shrugged.

What was she going to do when Davey came to? What was Hambone going to say?

"That's enough," someone said behind her. She spun around to see Hambone. He jerked the gun out of her hands. "Put those clothes away," he said to the women. They sank back down.

Davey woke up with a groan. He saw Hambone, scrambled to his feet, swayed, and put his hand against his head with a grimace. "Jesus Crisp," he said. "You see what letting her in has done?"

Hambone smiled with one corner of his mouth. "I see what she's done to you."

"She caught me with..."

"With your pants down? Big man like you, and she knocked you out cold."

Maybe this wasn't going to be so bad after all.

"Murdergirl, what am I going to do with you? You know the rules. You *know* how it all works. I don't make the rules, do I?"

She shook her head.

"And now here you are, encouraging these poor girls to break the rules. It's got to be bad enough having Davey up inside you all grunting and thrusting, now you've got them thinking about the moral side of it and if maybe there's some better way than getting fucked in the ass for food. Well," he said, "there *ain't.*" He spat on the dusty ground, his saliva black from the ash and bonemeal he had just been scrubbing his teeth with. "You two," he said to the other Bones, "show Murdergirl the door." He looked her in the eye. "Every day from you, complaints. You don't like how I do things. I get it. So spend a few weeks out there and see if that changes how you think about things in here."

"Wait, Hambone," she said. "I hear it. Let me stay. I already know what it's like out there." Sand. Sun. Teeth.

"Just like your mother." He grinned his big white grin and shook his head. "You need reminding."

The two men grabbed her shoulders and arms. "Get off of me!" she shouted. She struggled to break free, but together they were much stronger. They dragged her to the camp entrance, and pulled back the burlap door. She managed to kick one of them in the shin, and he let go, cursing. She wrenched her arm away from the other one and shook herself free. Fists up, she turned to face him, but before she could swing he put both hands on her shoulders and shoved, sending her tumbling over backwards out the entrance. She got to her feet. The two men stood in the entrance, Davey and Hambone behind them. "Hambone, please, let me..." she said, and stopped. Her shoulders slumped. "At least give me a weapon." The burlap folded across the doorway, shutting out the light from inside.

A moment later, it opened. Hambone tossed something out and closed the entrance again. A metal bar thudded into the sand in front of her. She picked it up. It looked like it had a hundred years' worth of rust caked on. She swung it through the air. At least it was heavy, and it seemed solid enough.

It was too early in the seasons to be cold at night, but late enough that it wasn't warm either. She started walking. She had to find shelter somewhere. In the dark there could be animals, or worse, humans—Skinheads—and she had no torch.

She looked back at the Bones' camp. Only a little light made it out, just a faint glow lighting up the smoke from the cooking flames as it rose into the night sky, and the tinkling laughter of the two women reached her. She turned and trudged away.

There had to be something out here, somewhere to hide from the night dangers. But there was nothing but sand and sun-baked dirt. Insects chirped and chittered, and unseen creatures skittered around her as she passed. Up and down dunes she went, over and over, with dark clouds covering the moon so she had no way to track time and know how long it had been.

A sound from the darkness. Barely there. Was that chortling breathing? A hyena. Her body went cold. A long time ago, hyenas hadn't lived in the Valley, but now the weather was just fine for them. She stood completely still. A hyena would happily eat you while you were still alive, your heart still pumping blood and you screaming with every bite. Blood pounded in her ears. She strained to hear. Was it still there? Sweat formed on her forehead and neck, cold sweat.

Her own breath was short, quick. She could not will it to change. She tightened a shaky grip on the metal bar. Even a zip-pistol would be better, but at least it was something. The darkness was quiet. Or was there laughter? Was the monster waiting, waiting for her to move, waiting for her to run, so it could pounce on her from behind?

A breeze rose. Did she feel the hot breath of the hyena? If she put out her hand, would she feel the hairy muzzle and the cruel teeth? Suddenly, she swung the metal bar, meeting only air. She hurled it with all her strength straight ahead, and then ran the opposite direction. The hair on the back of her neck told her she was in danger, that it was right behind. She ran until her lungs screamed at her, until she stumbled and went to her knees in the sand.

She sucked in air. There was no hyena. Or was there? Had there been? Impossible to tell, in the darkness. Skinheads could be watching her, waiting. A hyena den could be nearby. She got to her feet and kicked at the ground. There was nothing to do but walk, hoping for shelter.

The night was getting cool now; she had been walking for hours. Still there was nothing, and after the hyena she wasn't even sure what direction she was going in. In the daylight at least she'd be able to navigate by the sun, maybe the smoke from the Forge.

Out here, it wasn't hard to remember why she had joined the Bones. It was fine to want things a certain way, to dream about a better Valley, but when you were hungry, when it was dark and cold, when you had nothing and nobody, you needed other people, almost no matter who they were or what they stood for.

Murdergirl felt it must have been nearing the middle of the night. She stepped cautiously now, and listened for the grainy slithering of snakes in the sand. One sting from a cripple snake and she would spend hours or days in paralyzed agony until she died of thirst.

Her foot caught in something and she stumbled, almost falling to the ground. She went back and felt around in the sand. A long, rectangular box. Just big enough for a human. She drew her hand back and stood up. It was a coffin. Here? In the middle of nowhere? She tugged on her ponytail. If it was a coffin, if it had a person in it, there could be something she could use. She knelt back down and carefully felt around the edges of the box. Then she reached directly into the middle of it. Her hand hit the sandy wood at the bottom. It was empty. The lid, opened to the side, was a fine mesh. This had to be an abandoned Wormhole. She'd heard of, but never seen, the people called Worms. During the day, they lived in 'holes' they made themselves under the sand, and only came out at night. She opened and closed the lid. It was made of a dozen layers of the mesh, each holding a small amount of sand, and with the lid closed it looked and felt like just another tiny bump in the desert. It wasn't what she'd had in mind for shelter—a cave with a flame and a bucket full of corn, rather—but it was where she was going to spend the rest of the night. Presumably they'd made these things breathable. She slid into the box, found the inside handle for the lid, and pulled it shut. The general silence of the night was further muted. The air felt immediately hot from her body, but it was breathable. Something dangled from the lid and brushed against her face. She reached out and felt it with her hand. Some kind of mouthpiece. Of course. She fitted it into her mouth and took a cautious half-breath. Cool, fresh air entered her lungs. She let it fill her up. With her elbows, knees, and feet, she tested the limits of the box. It wasn't bad. It was warm and dry. There was enough room to turn over and wiggle your toes, not enough room to have a party. As she shuffled around, she felt something protruding near her bottom. She reached down and found another tube. She flattened it down so it wasn't poking her, and decided not to consider it further. Whatever that was for, she wasn't a Worm—she'd just open the lid if she needed to. With the sounds of occasional animals scuttling over the top, she drifted off to sleep.

Chapter 3

Murdergirl woke and choked on the thing in her mouth before remembering the mouthpiece. Wind howling above the surface had woken her. She could hear sand blowing by above. A sandstorm. She was lucky some Worm had abandoned his box—being in a sandstorm wouldn't kill you, but it'd make you wish you were dead. In the box, she could just wait it out.

She laughed against the breathing tube. Murdergirl Hawkins, in a box, breathing through a tube. When she was a kid, she hadn't necessarily had specific plans for the future, but even her vague plans didn't include anything like this. She'd thought maybe she would be part of a group doing… something. It didn't matter what, really. As long as it was more than just day-to-day survival. Even the Bones, in their way, were just surviving. How had she joined with them? Just trying to survive, same as anyone else. And when the price of full membership in the gang was to kill, to give up your name, she had barely hesitated. Well, that was the world.

Several grains of sand entered her mouth. She took out the mouthpiece and wiped them from her tongue with her fingers, then put the mouthpiece in again. More sand sprayed through the tube, dozens of grains. She jerked her mouth away and coughed. Sand coated the inside of her cheeks and stuck to her teeth. Her mouth was full of grit. She gathered as much of it as she could with her tongue and spat against the wall of the box. Something had gone wrong with the filtration system; the box was abandoned, who knew how old it might be? The air in the box was stale and tasted of her sweat. After a few minutes, she felt lightheaded from rebreathing the same air. Her lungs heaved to take in more air, but it wasn't enough. She might wish she was dead out there in the sandstorm, but that'd be better than actually being dead from suffocation.

She gently lifted the lid to have a look outside. The wind ripped it away from her, and sand poured into the box. She fought the instinct to gasp as the full force of the wind smashed into her; she pulled her vest up onto her head and pressed it right against her nose and mouth. At least she could breathe. A million grains of sand whipped against the bare skin of her back as she got to her knees, and she wished she'd asked for her long-sleeved shirt instead of that metal pipe.

A pebble cracked into her spine. "Fuck!" she screamed into the thick fabric. She gritted her teeth as sand stung the torn flesh. It wasn't safe to be there. If there was one pebble, there could be a whole rockfield nearby, and it would only take one a little larger than what had hit her to knock her unconscious. But where to go? She lowered the vest a few millimeters below her eyebrows and snuck a peek through squinted eyes. In the brown blindness of the storm, the only feature was sand, sand, sand. Walking directly into the storm was out of the question, so her only choice was to blindly walk with the wind at her back, naked from her chest to her hips. She went carefully, one foot placed in front of the other, feeling for safe footing in the ever-shifting sand. Sand filtered up into her hair against her scalp and filled the crack of her ass, already rubbing her skin raw with every step. The skin on her back and arms was numb from the constant assault against it. It had been years since there was a storm this bad—and she'd experienced that with shelter. Another pebble, thankfully smaller than the first, shot right against the boney point of her right elbow; the nerves screamed in pain all up and down her arm. If she ever saw Hambone again… her hand felt for the metal bar, and found nothing—she had thrown it at the hyena, now she had no weapon. But there was no point in thoughts like that anyway. Still, as she walked on legs already tired from a day and a night of walking, she thought them. One good crack across the mouth with a hunk of metal should get rid of that big white smile of his. Then she could shove it right up Davey's—

The sand went out from under her foot as she placed it down. She shifted her weight to her back foot and the sand went from under it as well. She overbalanced and pitched forward, sliding down a sand dune on her front. It was a high dune, and she slid for several seconds. She slowed to a stop and lay unmoving. The lee of the dune lessened the howl of the storm, though dust and sand still filled the air. She lifted her head an inch and pulled the vest down to get a look at her surroundings. Instantly, dust blew into her eyes. She closed her eyes, gritted her teeth, and struck out at nothing with a clenched fist.

A metallic clang greeted her fist. For a moment, she forgot about the sand in her eyes and everywhere else. She spread out her palm. Beneath a layer of wind-blown sand, there was metal. Conscious of sharp edges, she let her hand glide over it and discover its shape. It was a rectangle, and there was a handle. A door, in the middle of the desert. It would be nonsense if the door led anywhere. It had to have blown off some vehicle hundreds of years ago. She turned the handle and felt a bolt disengage. She pulled upwards, but nothing happened. It was too heavy. She stood up, vest held against her face. Anything would be better than being out here. Well, almost anything. If it was a pit where the Worms kept their snakes, it wouldn't be better. She needed two hands to open it and find out. She took a deep breath and pulled her vest down. Sand blew into her nostrils. She bent down, grabbed the handle with both hands, and pulled the door open. There was a hiss she could hear even over the sandstorm, and a brief rush of cool air against her skin. She found the handle on the opposite side of the door and gripped onto it to hold the door open. Moving her foot forward, searching, she found a step leading down. She brought her other foot forward and found the next step. Once more, and she stepped into empty space. She plummeted down, her eyes flew open, and she screamed into the sand-filled air. The door came down with her, her hands still holding tight to it. It slammed back into its frame and jolted her, leaving her swinging from the handle. She looked down, but it was pitch-black, no way to see what was below. A screw pinged out of the handle, and she dropped an inch. The handle bent with an ear-piercing squeal. If she was going to drop, she was going to do it when she chose. She let go.

Her boots clapped onto the concrete floor just a few inches below, jarring her bones. She stood still, quieted her breathing, and listened. It was quiet, it was dark, and—she hoped—it was safe.

Chapter 4

Her eyes adjusted to the darkness until it was just a shade lighter than completely black. A ladder just next to her led back up to the steps. She felt on the wall behind the ladder. There had to be some source of light—an oil lamp, a candle, a torch wrapped in rags, anything. Her hand found a plastic protrusion and she accidentally nudged it downwards. With a faint click, the room lit up. Her breath caught in her throat, and she turned around to see the single bulb hanging from the ceiling, glowing with the light of a hundred candles. Lectricity. She'd seen people do things that made lectric sparks, but this was something very different. It was a steady, solid light, with no flickering like a flame would have. Could there really have been a time when everyone had lights like these in their homes, in their pockets, and even outside to push away the night?

The room held further wonders. In one corner there was a bed from the before times. There were shelves piled with cans. She couldn't read the words on them, but the pictures of food told her enough. Most of the cans bulged, those were bad for you—poison. Why would someone poison food and then put it in a can? She picked a safe one—a very short can with a picture of a fish on it. A fish! She had never eaten a fish. Had anyone? Slimy beasts from a thousand years before, living in those impossible places where the water was so deep you couldn't see the bottom. They slithered, but they didn't need to breathe. She pulled the lid off using its ring and stuffed the pieces of fish into her mouth using her fingers. Tasty. Like a snake, but better.

She sucked the oily juice from her fingers and looked around the room. There were tables covered in things she'd never seen, more lectric things with wires, and tools of all kinds. In the middle of the room, still gleaming beneath a layer of dust, a motorcycle stood on supports so that its wheels were just an inch off the floor. She had played with ones like it when she was a child—but those were rusted and broken, with wheels that had nothing left on them but bent and crumbling metal. She went to it and stroked the leather seat, wiping the dust away. Motorcycles were supposed to move on their own, like some kind of animal, but they needed food too, and nobody knew what kind anymore.

She swung her leg over and straddled the seat. She put her hands on the handles and twisted them. "Broom, broom," she whispered. People said that was the noise it had made, back when it was alive. There were several things on the motorcycle, things you could push and things you could turn. She pushed and turned most of them, with no result. Then she turned a small metal one. The motorcycle growled below her, and she shot off to the side, knocking over a table and scattering everything on the floor. She crouched behind the table with her heart pounding in her chest. She forced herself to breathe, and she stood up. It was okay. It wasn't *really* an animal, it only did that when she turned the metal. She went back to it and turned the metal again. The motorcycle growled for a moment or two, deafening in the enclosed space, then spluttered before stopping with a small cough, like it was sick.

It needed food. All else forgotten, her eyes darted around. One of the shelves had bottles and cans of varying sizes, some with pictures of other motorcycles on them. Were any of them what it wanted? She stroked her hand across her chin while she scanned the possibilities, and smelled the fish she had eaten. That was it—if it had a place where food went in, she could smell that, smell the containers, and put the smells together. There was a large container—bigger than several barrels—on its side next to the shelf, with a red can in front of it. *G-a-s*. It was connected to some sort of machine that she now noticed a low rumble from, and occasional gurgling. Did it grow the food? She turned a valve on the large container, pouring some into the can. Its smell matched the motorcycle's. She poured a full can in, along with several other liquids she poured into their holes. It was all liquids, nothing solid. It didn't eat, it drank.

Getting the motorcycle up the ladder would be impossible, but somebody wouldn't have put it in there if there wasn't a way to get it out. She looked around the room. There were more doors. She opened one, finding more supplies—clothes, blankets. And the next only had more food. But the third door opened into a hallway, a little wider than the motorcycle and ten strides long, with another door at the end. She pushed the door at the other end, and it swung open with a protesting metal creak. Bright daylight hurt her eyes; she squinted and brought her hand up to shield them. The sandstorm had stopped, and a vast expanse of empty desert spread out below her. She stepped outside to see that the door opened halfway into the side of a gently sloped dune, where dead mesquite and saltbush camouflaged it. The outer side of the door was itself coated in some kind of sandy substance that blended perfectly into the dune. A human skeleton lay on the slope, a hole in the back of its skull. It was bleached white, but not so faded as bones that had been in the sun for years; the sandstorm might have only just uncovered it. It could have been there one year or a hundred.

Murdergirl tipped the motorcycle forward and rolled it off the stand. It listed to one side, and she had to fight to keep it upright. It was heavy, heavier than she was. At the end of the hallway, she stood and pulled on her ponytail. She smiled. Nobody could stop her. She mounted the motorcycle, balanced on the toes of her boots, and turned the metal. The motorcycle's roar filled the hallway behind her. "Broom, broom," she said, and twisted the handle. The motorcycle jumped out of the hall, almost jerking the handles from her hands, but she kept them gripped tightly. The motorcycle rolled down the hill. She involuntarily tightened her grip, squeezing the left handle, which brought it to a jerking stop that almost tossed her off. She rolled her shoulders and flexed her fingers on the handles. The arrow on the right handle pointed ahead. She twisted it and the motorcycle sprayed sand out from the rear wheel and darted forward. With steady pressure on the handle, she kept it going. The growl of the machine vibrated up deep inside her, and she wanted more. She twisted the handle, and the motorcycle between her legs responded powerfully. The needle in front pointed to four-zero. Her hair unfurled behind her like a banner. It felt impossible; no person could have ever gone this fast. She looked over her shoulder at the mesquite-door in the hill, already far in the distance. To the left and the right there were hills on the horizon; she wouldn't get lost as long as she didn't go past them. She grinned widely and pushed the handle farther forward. The needle climbed to six-zero. With her thighs gripping the beast, she urged it onward. She could do anything. She could go anywhere. "Woohoo!" she screamed to the sky, unable to hear it herself as the wind whipped her cry of joy away.

She saw a figure standing motionless on the ridge of a distant dune. They appeared the same color as the sand they stood on.

The ground became rougher, jolting her on the seat. She let up on the power, slowed down, and turned to go back where she came from. The wheel skidded and flipped sharply to the right and the motorcycle dropped to the ground, throwing her into the air. The motorcycle's engine died, and for a brief second there was no sound. Then the ground smacked into her and knocked the breath from her lungs. She bounced and rolled over and over in the sand. When she came to a stop, she rolled over on her back, gasping for air. Gradually, she was able to breathe normally. She moved her arms and legs, feet and hands. Nothing broken. She wiggled her fingers in the air and laughed out loud. The figure on the dune was gone, forgotten. She got to her feet and ran back to the motorcycle. What a ride!

Chapter 5

Murdergirl woke and sat up, immediately alert. She pushed the covers away. Whose bed was this? Then she remembered. It was hers. Whoever had put all this here, they hadn't been here in a long time—they probably weren't even alive anymore. She picked up a blanket and rubbed it between her fingers. She bounced her bottom on the bed. Just a day ago she'd been sleeping in an abandoned Worm-coffin and breathing sand.

She yawned, stretched, and stood up to make the bed. People used to do this every morning, and they were safe and warm, so instead they worried about things like… like she didn't even know what. What could you worry about if you had everything? Maybe people in the before times never worried.

To pull the blanket up to the top of the bed, she lifted the pillows. She jerked back, startled. A half-length shotgun lay underneath, its weight pressing into the sheet. Its dark metal gleamed in the lectric light. This was a real gun, made in a real factory that used to exist somewhere. Some people still made guns, like the zip-pistols the Bones had, and most of the time they worked, but sometimes they misfired or didn't fire at all, and you could tell by looking at them that someone who didn't really know how to make a thing had made them. She'd only ever seen one real old gun; Hambone had it and cared for it like it was his own child.

Hambone. While she was here eating anything she wanted and sleeping in a soft bed, the Bones were taking food that wasn't theirs, leaving those in the rest of the Valley hungry. Her hand went to the butt of the gun. She felt the sleek metal and closed her fingers around it. She hefted it up. It was heavier than it looked, as it should be—something that could kill should have a weight to it, should make you think about it. Everyone said that if you were stronger, you did what you wanted and that was just the way things were. She could use this to be a lot stronger, stronger than a dozen men, and that would be just the way things were.

She slung her leg over and gave the beast the power it wanted. The desert raced away beneath her. Every month after the Bones went to the Garden, they went to the Oasis. It was a smaller operation; they were only after wine and maybe a woman, if any were willing, so there would probably only be about six Bones there.

She was still bruised and sore from yesterday's crash. This time, she kept the speed around three-zero, just over a quarter of what the needle could go to. The speed was still exhilarating. People had always gone this fast—and faster!—in the before time. After a few minutes, she found the path. From the Bones' camp to the Oasis was a half-day's journey on foot if you started early. But on the motorcycle, it was only twenty minutes more before she could see the trees on the horizon. Soon she was entering the Oasis. Trees as tall as twenty people stood all around in every direction. The people of the Oasis said the trees had been there since the beginning of time. Their limbs were bare and they were grey like skeletons. It was quiet in the Oasis, just like everywhere else, but there it was different because at one point it would have been full of life. If you pulled up one tiny plant in the desert now, a hundred insects scurried in every direction—how much life could the trees have supported in their turn? But the same thing that killed everything else had killed the trees too, and left them standing as a reminder of what used to be.

She rode up the path directly toward where the people of the Oasis lived. Here, in the middle of many thousands of dead trees, there was a large clearing where the sun could get through, and a little water came up from below the ground. Among the green plants and vines and the twenty or so little huts made from limbs that the trees had dropped, the Bones' cart stood. This one was small enough that two people could move it, both of them pushing the bars at the sides. It was already loaded with several dozen plastic jugs filled with wine. Nobody knew how to make anything out of plastic anymore, but there were so many plastic things left from before that they would never run out.

There was no way to sneak up on them; the beast would not be silenced. As she came closer, the Bones and all the people of the Oasis came to see what the noise was. Most of the adults stood well back near their huts, and the children stood near the adults.

Like she had thought, there were six Bones, including Murderboy. They clustered around the cart. She stopped twenty steps in front of them and let the machine gently rumble. All of them probably knew what it was, they had all seen a thousand and more dead machines. But to know what something was, that was one thing, and to see it, to hear it, to feel it vibrate in your chest, that was something you couldn't be prepared for. She gave it power while holding the brake, and it roared, wanting to be set free. The Bones and all of the Oasis drew back, and children hid behind adults. Two of the Bones took zip-pistols from their waistbands. Tobas was one of them. He called out something she couldn't hear; she could only see his mouth moving in the middle of his red beard. She turned the metal and stepped off the motorcycle. The Oasis and the trees beyond were silent. A light wind moved through and rattled the branches of the huts.

"Murdergirl, what are you doing here?" Tobas called out again, his voice unnaturally loud. "You're not a Bone anymore. Get out." He gestured away with his zip-pistol.

Her hand automatically went as if to tug her ponytail, but instead she went for the concealed shotgun strapped to her back. She aimed it at him. The people of the Oasis all stepped back again, behind and into their huts. She started to give the speech she had practiced on the way, and her voice caught in her throat. She cleared it. "All of you, Bones, hear this, and *you* get out. These people aren't yours. The Oasis, the Garden, the Forge—all of the people and the things they make don't belong to you."

"You're going to get yourself killed," Murderboy called out to her. His zip-pistol still stuck out of his waistband. "You know the Bones don't mess around."

"Messing around is what me and you have been doing," she called back. "Do you really want to keep on this way? Hurting people who are weak, eating food you didn't grow, fucking people even when they say no?"

Murderboy shrugged. Tobas whipped his zip-pistol up, and without time to think she pulled the trigger on the shotgun. An explosion louder even than the motorcycle kicked the butt of the shotgun back into her stomach. Tobas' zip-pistol weakly fired off into the trees. Dark red patches appeared on his vest. He dropped to his knees, hands trying and failing to keep his blood inside. He looked at her with a questioning expression, and then fell back, dead.

Sickness rose up from her stomach, but she forced it down. Her hands shook on the gun and she fought to catch her breath. She pointed it at the other Bone, who still held his zip-pistol. He dropped it like it had burned him. Her throat was dry. "Go back to your camp," she said, in a voice suddenly hoarse. "Tell Hambone what I said." Two of the Bones went to the bars on the cart. "Leave it," she commanded. They looked uncertainly at each other, and then obeyed. All of the Bones walked up the path, back towards the desert, and she was alone with the people of the Oasis.

Chapter 6

She put the shotgun on her back. It pressed her vest against her sweat-soaked skin. She walked to the cart, and Tobas lying near it. His legs had bent under him, and his eyes stared up at her. *Why?* his face asked her. She looked up at the people who stood at a distance from her. "You're free," she said. "Take the things off the cart, they're yours. Still, they only looked at her. "What are you waiting for? What's the matter?"

A blond-haired man with a full beard stepped forward. "Who are you?" She saw him looking at the clothes she wore, which matched those on Tobas' bloody corpse. "What group are you with?"

"I'm not with anybody else. I'm Murdergirl."

She saw some of them mouthing her name. *Murdergirl?* She could give them the name she'd been born with, but anybody who that meant something to was dead. "Hawkins," she said. "Murdergirl Hawkins." She looked at the man. "And you, what's your name?"

"Stevenson," he answered. "What do you want from us?"

They didn't understand at all. It was for them that she had done it. "I don't want anything. I came to free you. You don't have to be afraid of the Bones anymore. You don't have to give them your work."

Stevenson pointed to the dead Bone. "You did this to free us?"

She nodded. He shook his head and said, "This dead man won't help anything. You've only made things worse for us. Do you think the Bones won't come back, but this time with thirty men? We live by the sweat of our bodies, and the Bones allow us to keep doing it if we give them some of what we make. It's hard living, but we live."

"But you don't have to. You could stop them. You could fight, like I'm doing."

"Look around you." He gestured at the people behind him. "Do we look like warriors? Like I said, we *live*. We don't kill."

Of the probably f people, about half were women. Fifteen were children, and ten were old. "With guns..." she started, and trailed off.

"Exactly. With what guns?" He pointed at her shotgun. "That's the only real gun I've seen in my thirty years." He waved the back of his hand at her. "The Bones are strong, and they're willing to kill over a jug of wine. Better to give them the wine, and live."

"If we worked together—"

"No! There's no chance. You want us to risk our lives, the lives of our families, our women, our children, our parents, the whole Oasis, just so the Bones can't get drunk anymore?"

The sick rose up in her throat. She had killed a man, and for what? Nothing had changed.

"It's more than that." She had to make him understand. "The weak, they don't have to give in to the strong. And just because someone is strong, what does that mean?" Her voice was raised so she was almost shouting. Why couldn't they hear? "And if they take the wine, and drink it, does that make it theirs?"

"It doesn't matter who's wine it is," Stevenson said. "We cannot fight the Bones. We will not fight the Bones. You ask too much, and barely understand your own question. So you have a gun. And you kill, just like the Bones. Now go." He kicked sand at her. "Go!"

Stevenson turned to the people nearest him. "Get a dozen more jugs," he said, "we need to be ready for them when they come back."

She opened her mouth, but stopped. Her shoulders sagged. They wouldn't listen. Maybe they couldn't.

Why was the world this way now? She looked out into the desert, where she had been riding since she left the Oasis. Maybe the world was always this way, even before. The strong taking anything they wanted, with the weak as their slaves. There had been wars in the before time, wars where more people than she could ever count had died. Some people said that a war had been the end of it all—a war with weapons so destructive they had killed even the ones that used them.

She looked down at the motorcycle. It wasn't people with guns who had made machines like it, and so many other machines. They had used their brains, and their hands, and they had worked together. She'd seen pictures of the old cities. Filled with so many people, and houses taller even—much taller—than the trees at the Oasis. It wasn't people with guns who had done that. Everybody had worked together. But something had gone wrong, something had messed up the whole beautiful machine. Now it was dead; lifeless, like the corpse of a desert creature. Men like Hambone, they grew on its corpse like a fungus, and without the machine to stop them they grew out of control, until now they thought they *were* the machine, that they kept the world rolling.

While she thought, she had let off the power handle. The motorcycle had rolled to a stop, and she balanced it with one boot on the sand. Flames got rid of fungus. If you burned it all out, it couldn't grow anymore.

The Bones' camp was far away on foot, but she could be there in a few minutes. She gave the motorcycle power.

Chapter 7

The Tomb Tree stood tall and silent as she rode past. She would end this today. Without Hambone, the Bones would be no more. Then there were the Skinheads, and then the entire valley would be free. Without them standing in the way, the people could start to rebuild the machine.

The Bones' camp came up quickly from the horizon. She still wasn't used to the motorcycle's speed; you got everywhere faster than you thought. She circled the camp, letting the sound of the motorcycle penetrate into it. At the entrance to the camp, she stopped. "Hambone!" she called out, and gave the beast full power. Its roar drowned out even the wind. Hambone strode outside, flung the burlap gate aside, Davey following him. Five or six other of the Bones came out as well, and spread along the front of the camp. Murderboy stood just inside the entrance, holding the burlap aside. Hambone grinned his big white grin and said something that couldn't be heard. His grin shrank a little, and he shouted, but the motorcycle still overpowered his voice. He closed his eyes and set his jaw, took in a deep breath, and then Murdergirl turned off the metal, catching him with his mouth open ready to shout again. As silence surrounded them, Hambone's grin returned.

"Well, well, well. Look at this." He flung out his hands, indicating Murdergirl and the motorcycle. "What have you brought us, Murdergirl? Or..." he removed his hat and bowed his head, "...it's not Murdergirl anymore, is it?" He grinned wider. "I'm sure Tobas would be pleased to know it was he who had the honor of giving you your name back."

"I'm still Murdergirl."

He placed his hat back on his head. "And why is that?"

She pulled the shotgun off her back. "I haven't had the kill I want yet."

Hambone nodded his head gently, feeling the rhythm of some music only he could hear. "Oh, boys, do you hear that?" He looked at Davey. "Mmm, didn't I tell you?"

Davey frowned. "Hambone..." he started, but said nothing else, only took one step away from the bigger man.

Hambone put his hands up in the air and swayed. "After what happened, you said no woman could really be a Bone." He looked into the sky, as if talking to someone there. "And now, look here, if it ain't nobody but our Murdergirl, here to challenge for the throne, and tell me if that's not me in her."

"I don't want your throne." She pointed the shotgun at him. She made eye contact with Murderboy, standing just a step or two behind Hambone. *Help me,* she mouthed. He shook his head, and stepped out of sight.

"My, my." Hambone stroked his hand over the pistol at his hip. He smacked his lips. "Ain't this a tasty situation?"

"It's not one of your games, Hambone!" she shouted.

He whipped the gun out of his waistband and aimed it at her, finger ready on the trigger. "Then how come I'm winning it, girl? Look at it. There's eight of us here, and forty more inside. And you?" He leaned to the left and right, as if he was looking behind her. "Who do you got?"

She turned the metal, and the motorcycle started with a steady growl. When she turned the handle and it suddenly roared louder, one of the Bones jumped. She had the shotgun, and she had the beast.

"Enough of this!" Davey shouted, and snatched the pistol out of Hambone's hand.

Murdergirl swiveled toward Davey and pulled the trigger at the same time he pulled the trigger of the pistol. Then, it seemed like there was all the time in the world. She couldn't see it, but their shots crossed paths. The balls of shot filled Davey's body and made the burlap behind him fly up. She felt something like a punch combined with a cramp in her stomach. There was time to consider what it might be, even though she already knew. She put her hand to her stomach and looked down to see blood trickling through her fingers and a dark red patch spreading on her vest. She looked up; Hambone advanced toward her. With her hand still at her stomach, she turned the metal and gave the beast power. It lurched at Hambone, spitting sand out behind, and he dove out of the way. The motorcycle shot forward into the camp, and the wooden supports of the front wall gave way with a crack. A woman sat up, open-mouthed, with a blanket clutched to her breasts, and the two men with her scrambled for their zip-pistols. Murdergirl brought her bloody hand up to the other handle and turned towards the men, causing them to jump and stumble and trip. One of them knocked over a burn barrel, sending a cascade of sparks and flame rolling along the ground and into the air. She went straight through the camp, dragging burlap behind her, and heard more wooden supports snapping. A gunshot exploded into the air, and she knew a bullet from a zip-pistol had missed her. She twisted the power handle and the beast roared, carrying her away into the desert.

Wind screamed around her. After several minutes, she realized she was safe. They could never catch her on foot. She smiled at the power of the beast she rode. Then a wetness on her thighs reminded her of what had happened. She looked down to see blood now soaking her pants, and her smile slipped away. Her head didn't want to stay upright. Could she get to the bunker? It was over there, past the Tomb Tree. Was that the Tomb Tree? It was hard to see from the sandstorm. The wind died down as the motorcycle coasted to a stop. Was there a sandstorm? She couldn't feel any sand, but she couldn't see beyond her own feet. She was losing herself. Losing everything. She slapped a bloody handprint onto her face, stinging pain to bring her back. If you're bleeding, you have to stop it. You have to stop the bleeding, then clean the wound, then patch it up.

She staggered off the motorcycle, forgetting to set its stand. It tipped over and knocked her to her knees. She slowly sucked in a breath and put her hands in the cool sand, sand that should be hot from the sun. The sky was dark. How long had she been kneeling there? Stars spun overhead. A circle of red sand shone beneath her. Stop the bleeding. She took her vest off and tipped over onto her side. The desert was cool against her cheek, and she was going to die. Her vision had cleared. She could see for miles; cool, clean desert, and the pool of darkness above. The sweet song of the crevice crickets surrounded her, being the only sound other than her breathing. She lay there, bleeding, and knew nobody could expect anything else of her. She didn't have to stop the Bones, didn't have to liberate the Valley. Didn't even have to stand up, because she couldn't. More of her life trickled out and stained the sand. She didn't have to be Murdergirl anymore, didn't have to take life in order to save life. Shapes appeared around her, rising from the desert itself. Rough, gritty hands grabbed her, picked her up. The desert took her. She accepted it, and breathed out.

Chapter 8

The air was hot.

"Give her water." An old woman's voice.

"But it's a waste. Others are thirsty." A girl.

"Harissa, when you have seen the moon circle the valley one hundred thousand times, then you can decide who drinks and who does not."

The girl huffed. Murdergirl felt the lip of a cup at her mouth, and a trickle of cold water. She drank, and the water cooled her inside.

"If the others find her—"

"Hush your foolishness, child. When she helped you, do we know what that cost her? Did we ask?"

The air was hot. The day was bright.

A cup at her mouth again. Murdergirl drank, and as she drank, the cup tipped up and the trickle became a stream. When she finished, she opened her eyes. "Thank you," she whispered. The world came into focus. The girl, Harissa, was leaned over her, and nodded acceptance. They were in a tent made of thick, white cactus fibers woven into a rough canvas, so there was shade, but the sun shining on the white canvas was enough to hurt your eyes. Murdergirl turned her head and saw Rebecca sitting on a bamboo chair. Without the old woman's help, she would have bled to death in the desert, or roasted in the sun. "Thank you for bringing me here," she said to Rebecca.

"Not us," the old woman replied. "The desert brought you here." Those hands that lifted her…

"We found you outside the Garden several days ago," Rebecca continued, "unconscious, bloody, almost dead."

"But you didn't die," Harissa said. "Can you walk?"

Murdergirl flexed her toes and shrugged. "Maybe," she said. "I'll try." She moved to slide her legs off the bed.

Rebecca put a wrinkled hand on Murdergirl's shoulder to stop her. "Harissa, enough."

Harissa folded her arms.

"I'm sorry," Murdergirl said. "Is something wrong?"

"You have nothing to be sorry for. Harissa, apologize."

"What do you think the Bones will do to us if they find her?"

"This woman…" Rebecca began, then said, "I'm sorry, what is your name?"

"Murdergirl."

Rebecca briefly lifted one eyebrow. "Murdergirl is our guest. We help her as…" She looked at Harissa expectantly.

"As the desert helps us all," Harissa finished.

Rebecca smiled and the lines of her face lit up. "Very good."

"We heard about what you did," Harissa said to Murdergirl, "What do *you* think the Bones would do if they found you here?"

Murdergirl considered. She could point out there wasn't any literal prohibition on killing a Bone. But Hambone wouldn't mess around. Best to be honest. "He'd kill someone," she said. "But it would probably be me. He would beat up some of you…" she looked at Harissa, "…except for the pretty ones, who might wish for that."

Harissa made a face and pulled her arms closer to her body.

"Nothing like that is going to happen," Rebecca said. "Hambone doesn't know Murdergirl is here. And if the Bones come, we've got their stock of food all ready, so they're not going to be snooping."

"And besides," Murdergirl said, "I've got my..." she trailed off, remembering that she didn't have her shotgun. The gun lay in the desert, and the beast lay with it, dying. Someone would find it, but they would use up its fuel quickly and then it would lay again, dead.

Rebecca reached under Murdergirl's pillow. "Is this what you mean?" She hefted the shotgun out and held it to her.

Murdergirl hesitantly reached for the shotgun. They had left it with her the whole time? She closed her fingers around it, savoring the weight of the cold metal.

"It's loaded," Rebecca said. "You never know what situation may arise."

Murdergirl turned on her side and tucked it back under her pillow. "What about—"

"The motorcycle? The desert brought that too. Now, *can* you walk?"

"Rebecca!" Harissa protested.

The old woman smiled. "It's okay to ask when your motives are kind. Our guest must be hungry, perhaps she would like to come for food."

Murdergirl's mouth watered and her saliva glands ached. She hadn't eaten anything since her confrontation with the Bones, maybe a week ago. As she slid her legs to the side of the bed, the muscles of her abdomen complaining as she did. She reached her hand down to the pain, expecting to feel bandages, but instead she felt wetness, and her fingertips came back covered in green and white slime. She pushed the covers down to see that there was no dressing at all on her bullet wound; it was an open hole in her stomach, with a thick gunk that had oozed out of it. She looked at Rebecca questioningly.

"It's better this way," Rebecca said. "The desert air is the best healer. Your body needs to breathe. If you cover your mouth with a cloth, is it easier or harder to breathe?"

Murdergirl shrugged her shoulders. "The Gardeners are healers," she said, accepting it. "I'm a Bone. Or I was. I don't know what I am."

Rebecca waved the problem away. "Bone, Worm, Gardener, Skinhead, we all bleed the same, we all need the same. For today, just be Murdergirl."

Murdergirl smiled and gently eased her legs off the bed. What did it mean to be Murdergirl? She stood up carefully. Rebecca stood nearby, offering her shoulders, but Murdergirl wasn't going to use a woman over twice her age as a walking support. At the first step she took, her knee gave way and she stumbled, wincing and sucking air between her teeth as pain shot through her stomach.

"Don't be stubborn," Harissa said. "Rebecca's stronger than she looks."

The old woman cackled. "This passes for a compliment with her generation."

Murdergirl put her arm around Rebecca's bent shoulders, her stomach still complaining. The old woman's head barely came up to Murdergirl's shoulders herself, which put her at the perfect height to support the younger woman's weight.

Harissa pushed the canvas opening aside to let them pass. Murdergirl squinted and shielded her eyes as they adjusted to the blazing sun. It took a moment to focus more than a few paces away. Among a scattering of white tents, dozens of people were hard at work. Two men carried a large basket between them; it was piled with fruits, some which Murdergirl had never seen before. Two women sat weaving the white cactus fibers into canvas. A man walked with a plastic jug of water, taking care with each step as he carried the precious liquid. Others were busy patching holes in canvas and twining bamboo together.

Why couldn't everyone else work together like this? The Bones and the Skinheads, they took and took and took, so everyone else had to work twice as hard. The people in the Garden and the Oasis and the Forge were probably only a quarter of all the people in the Valley, but they supported themselves and the others with food and drink and flame. It wasn't always like that; she knew it couldn't have been. The motorcycle, the shotgun, plastic bottles, the ruined skeletons of the buildings far in the distance that stood even above the mountains, they were all proof of that. People couldn't make all that if they were busy planting figs and weaving canvas, crippling their hands with the same work over and over again.

A small stream, narrow enough to easily step over, ran through the middle of the camp, ending in a tiny pond you could lay across and still have dry scalp and toes, and shallow enough that it might not even get your ankles wet if you stood in it. Along the stream and around the pond, trees of every description grew. Except for the times, once or twice a year, when the sky suddenly dumped water on the desert and the desert just as quickly drank it up,

Murdergirl had never seen running or even standing water. The pond drew her towards it, but Rebecca stopped her with a firm hand on her chest.

"Sit," Rebecca directed her. Murdergirl sat at a small, round table, with three chairs. Like every other thing people made, big or small, they were made of roughly cut bamboo stalks twined together with bamboo fibers.

"Eat." On the table there was a large bowl of fruit, filled with bright red tanh fruit, prickly cactus nut, grapes fresh and dried, fresh green figs, palm dates, and several other fruits she didn't recognize. Her stomach rumbled and then cramped, she winced and bent forward.

"Almost a week without food," Rebecca said. "Start small."

Murdergirl used her fingertips to pick up a brown cactus nut about the size of her palm, being careful of the pricks. On the outside, it looked like something that didn't want you to eat it and that you shouldn't eat anyway, with its cracked skin and dozens of spikes. With fingertips of both hands, she twisted in opposite directions, and the nut came apart at its middle seam, showing bright pink skin on the inside and a soft, white flesh dotted with several black seeds about the size of her little fingernail. She dug two fingers in and pulled out some of the creamy flesh with a couple of seeds, and popped it into her mouth. She closed her eyes and savored. But not for too long, because she wanted more. Slowly, she moved from one fruit to the next, taking small bites, trying pieces handed to her by Rebecca and Harissa. And while she ate, they talked, with the sound of the tiny stream trickling towards the pond.

"It isn't as bad as some people might make you think," Rebecca said, "being a Gardener. Yes, the work is hard. And yes, it's hot. Yes, your back hurts, your feet hurt, your hands hurt. Your skin burns if you don't cover it, and you boil when you do cover it. And when you've done all that, somebody like Hambone or the Skinheads take half or more of what you've made."

Murdergirl waited. Rebecca popped a date into her mouth and chewed.

"You don't have to do anything you don't want. You're feeding people, like the desert feeds you." She reached out and patted Harissa on the shoulder; the girl continued staring off into the distance. "You can be around those you love. You can teach the young what's best."

"But you're working for someone else," Murdergirl said. "It's like being an aphid."

Harissa turned to the conversation and sat forward in her chair.

"Nature created the aphid and the ant," Rebecca said. "Is it better to be an ant?" She shrugged, palms upturned.

"This is stupid," Harissa said, which brought a smile to Rebecca's face. "We're people, not insects. And we know all the others are taking the things we make, aphids don't even have thoughts about it."

"It's not a bad life, is it?" The old woman replied. "Anyone in the Garden can leave if they want, yet we all choose to stay. What are the options? A person can wander in the desert, and die quickly on their own." Her eyes flicked to Murdergirl. "You can join up with someone like Hambone, killing people and taking from them."

"There's another," Harissa said.

Rebecca nodded her head slightly.

"We can fight," the girl continued. "We can fight, like Murdergirl. Right now, we could go, surprise them, maybe kill Hambone and stop them all." She made eye contact with Murdergirl, eyebrows raised, searching her, questioning her. *Could we fight? Could we kill? Could we win?*

Rebecca smiled and shook her head. "To be young again."

"It's not because I'm young! Murdergirl is old too, she did it."

Rebecca laughed. "Perhaps Murdergirl does not think she is so old. I know you don't like to hear it, but there is a benefit to being old. You have seen many things, done many things, and so you can see which way is best. But," she added, "of course there is also a benefit to being young. You haven't seen things, you haven't done things, so sometimes you accidentally find the best way."

"It's true that people can fight," Rebecca continued. "We can fight, we can kill. We can even tear apart the bodies of our enemies, like the Skinheads. When they do so, they make themselves less human. Today, somewhere under our feet in this camp, a thousand ants may have slaughtered another thousand and cut their bodies in half. Hambone is an ant, and that's not better than being an aphid. It's still not human."

"Then why did you let Murdergirl keep the gun? You could have buried it."

"I'm old," Rebecca said. "Who knows why I do things sometimes?"

Harissa huffed and looked at Murdergirl for support. Murdergirl put her hand to her stomach, feeling the tender flesh around her wound. She bit into a date. Now Davey was dead. She hadn't even wanted to kill him, but it was her finger on the trigger. Two people she had killed for nothing, and Hambone wouldn't let her get so close the next time.

She swallowed, the fruit going down in a hard lump that hurt her throat.

"I don't think it works anymore," she said. "They made the whole world one machine, every part of it in harmony. But something broke. Even if we killed Hambone, that wouldn't fix it. Another Bone would take over."

Rebecca raised her finger. "And that's even if we win. Let's say we all went, all of the Gardeners. The Bones are vicious, you know that. They could kill all of us. And then what has been gained?"

"At least we wouldn't be their slaves anymore," Harissa said.

Rebecca shook her head. "You're right, that would be something. But," she reached out and squeezed the girl's cheek, "I would rather you be alive, all the same."

Harissa rolled her eyes.

Chapter 9

Murdergirl followed Harissa. Or Harissa followed her; with how close the girl stayed to her in the week or so since she'd been up and about, it was hard to tell who was doing the following.

"You're going to love this," Harissa said.

"What is it? Where are we going?"

Harissa put her finger to her lips and shushed Murdergirl. They were just at the edge of the Garden, nobody else was around. Harissa looked around and motioned for Murdergirl to follow her. They walked out into the desert. About a hundred yards from the Garden, Murdergirl stopped to look back. Rolling sand dunes now disguised the Garden, no tents or trees could be seen; only their footsteps in the sand, in a wide, arcing path, told the way back. If a person didn't already know how to get there, they would only find the Garden by chance.

"Almost there," Harissa said, "come on."

As they walked now, Harissa changed to a strange, lilting gait. "Walk like this," she said, and pointed back to their footsteps. She walked as if she had a limp, then she skipped, and sometimes swept her foot to the side. Murdergirl did her best to copy, and when she glanced back, their footsteps did not make a definite path. A little while farther on, Harissa stopped and held up her hand. Murdergirl stopped. They were on top of a small dune, which was about chest high above the level ground.

"We have to wait," the girl said.

"Wait for what?"

Harissa turned slowly in a circle. "For anybody who might see." She pointed out at the horizon. "Watch and wait."

They watched, and they waited. Harissa slowly turned, and Murdergirl did too. Out in the desert, there was nothing but sand. Just when Murdergirl was about to suggest as much, Harissa stopped. She slid down the dune, motioning for Murdergirl to follow. Harissa plunged her hand into the side of the dune up to her elbow. She looked up, eyes closed, tongue at the corner of her mouth as she concentrated. Then she found what she was looking for and pulled. A hatch of sand layered on corrugated metal lifted away from the dune and revealed a narrow bamboo tunnel sloping down into the darkness.

"Quickly, in," Harissa said, crawling into the tunnel herself. Murdergirl followed, gently lowering the hatch behind. The light disappeared completely, but the tunnel was narrow enough that Murdergirl could feel every part of it as she crawled and swayed from side to side. The walls were smooth when they brushed her shoulders and hips, and the ceiling was also smooth against her head, while the floor was rough on her hands and knees.

Here, under the desert, it seemed as if there was nothing. The only sounds were Harissa shuffling ahead of her, and in the distance, the trickle of the Garden's stream. The Garden itself seemed far away, and the Bones even farther. Yet, even far away, Hambone and the others were no doubt preparing another raid. It had been several weeks since the last one, and their food would be running low. They could all stop and join one of the growing communities like the Garden, but they never would. There was something inside of them that told them they must have power, even if it was only the power to take fruit from someone who had grown it themselves. Was that thing new, or had it always been inside humans? Before the machine broke, had there been people standing at the top of those buildings that were now just skeletons, and had that same thing been whispering to them that they were masters of the world?

Down, down. The trickling was louder now, no longer just a trickle, and Harissa's shuffling was gone. Murdergirl's sight was gone, her sense of hearing and touch told her it was just her there, tunneling through, making her way to the deep center of the desert.

What made the Bones believe they were the masters? They had the same bodies as any other person, and the same minds. Except they had the ability to shut off the part of their mind that told them they were the same as other people, that all humans were their brothers and sisters, or maybe that part never existed, maybe they were born alone and they lived alone in their mind, separate from all of humanity and so able to believe they could be above it. And she had even believed the same about herself. When she killed Davey and Tobas, she wasn't thinking of them as her brothers with their own thoughts, feelings, hopes, dreams. The shotgun had given her power, and that power had made her separate.

She could see Harissa in front now, silhouetted by a faint circle of blue light. As they crawled nearer, the light brightened. The tunnel was still bamboo on every side, rough on the bottom, smooth on the rest. How far had they come; how long had this tunnel taken to dig? The sound of the stream filled her ears now, a sound that was an impossibility.

Harissa slipped out the end of the tunnel. Murdergirl followed, her legs stiff from the long crawl, but immediately forgot that as the sound smashed into her, sounding like a rainstorm and a sandstorm at the same time. The water! She searched for the word in her mind as her eyes took it in. The long-forgotten word. *River.* The tunnel had dropped them out into a cave as high as ten people and wide enough for the whole Garden to fit inside. Through the middle flowed a river of perfectly clear water, wider across than two people stretched out, and it looked deeper than she was tall. Strange, glowing plants grew on cracks and crevices in the rock walls, spreading a blue light all around and reflecting off the surface of the river back onto the ceiling and walls of the cave.

At one end of the cave, the water flowed down a cascade of rock, and out the other end at a low exit. The water rushed past, never stopping on its journey to wherever. She walked closer, feeling a tightness in her throat and tears stinging her eyes. How many times in her life had she been thirsty, lips cracked and throat parched, skin baked by the sun, wanting nothing other than a mouthful of water, and here there was so much, an endless supply, enough for a thousand people and a thousand more and still more. She stepped to the edge, legs trembling, and dropped to her knees. The air in the cave was cool, and close to the water it was cold like night. She dipped her hand into the river and up to the middle of her forearm. Her breath caught in her throat; it was cold like nothing she had ever felt, and there was power in the water. It pulled against her arm as it flowed. It was so cold on her arm that it became hot.

She looked back over her shoulder at Harissa. "It's amazing," she said.

Harissa pointed to her ear and shook her head.

"It's amazing!" Murdergirl shouted, laughing, and Harissa laughed with her, nodding her head.

This water could give life to everyone in the valley ten times over. The dead trees of the Oasis could flourish. Everyone could grow their own food, not just in the Garden. But the desert and the cave trapped the water below, there was no way to get it up. It was beautiful, but hidden away from everyone. As the river rushed by, she could see glimpses of her face reflected in the cool, blue light.

She cupped her hand under the surface and pulled up a handful of water to her mouth. Even the smell of the water had something wonderful about it, something that she craved. She drank it up, then drank several handfuls more.

Harissa had moved close by, and now stood, silently. Murdergirl sat back and looked at her. Harissa held a small, half-full bottle of water. In the cave's light, the water was blue.

"Do you want to be a part of the Garden?" Harissa asked, barely audible over the rushing water.

Murdergirl wiped the back of her hand across her dripping mouth. A part of the Garden. She had been part of the Bones, and it had only been unhappiness and murder. But in the Garden, and here, in the cave, it could be different. She nodded her head.

"Will you help others, as the desert helps us all?" Harissa's voice was louder now, as clear as the water in the bottle.

Murdergirl looked up at her. The young girl's hair blazed a reddish blue, like the hottest flames.

"I will," she whispered, the words drowned by the river.

Harissa tipped Murdergirl's head back. Clear, blue water poured from the bottle onto her forehead. Icy rivulets soaked her hair, blurred her eyes, ran down her face, into her ears, pattered off her vest and splashed onto the hard rock below.

"As the water flows over you," Harissa recited, "it takes your form. It accepts you."

Murdergirl closed her eyes. She opened her mouth and accepted the water. It was possible to be a part of the world, not separate from it, not on top of it, but one with it. In the cave, she was part of it, she was inside it. It would help her, and she would help others, who were all part of the world.

The stream turned to a trickle and then a drip. The last drop fell onto her face. The empty bottle dropped to the ground and bounced. She opened her eyes and looked up at Harissa. From her sitting position, the girl towered over her. Murdergirl drew in a deep breath through her nose, taking in the cool, clean air of the cave, the smell of the water and the smell of her own sweat. She smiled.

Chapter 10

Prickly greasewood bulbs sat several inches under the surface, spreading out a vast root network, taking water from Garden trees. With poisonous roots and no fruit, greasewood was a pest plant.

Murdergirl slipped her hand into the sand, feeling around for the first prick of a bulb through the protective palm leaf slivers that wrapped her hand. When she found it, she curled her fingers around the base of the bulb and tugged. She felt the pop, and the bulb, half the size of her closed fist, came away in her hand. Greasewood bulbs were good for nothing except the small amount of black paste from the pulped bulb flesh which could be used for decoration. She tossed it onto the pile of about fifty she had pulled that morning. After a few days, more bulbs would grow and need to be pulled.

Even under her headscarf, the sun baked her head. She put her back against a nearby date palm tree and slid down for a much-needed rest. Her hands, wrapped in palm slivers and soothed with precious aloe oil, still ached and complained of blisters.

Hux sat against the trunk next to her. Tall, and with skin darker than hers, it took him a lot longer to burn in the sun, so he didn't wear a headscarf. His pile of greasewood bulbs was bigger than hers four times again.

"How do you go so fast?" she asked.

He held his hand out to her. "Feel it."

She pulled her fingertips along his palm, which was bare, not wrapped like hers. Thick callouses covered it, rough as the tree bark behind her head.

He smiled. "Twenty-five years of gardening is how."

Murdergirl took a drink from her bottle, and her arm protested from the motion. Twenty-five years? Two days had nearly killed her.

"I was born here," Hux continued, "and here I am still. My mother brought me into the desert right there." He pointed to the pool in the middle of the Garden. Murdergirl lowered her bottle, a mouthful of water still unswallowed.

He smiled again. "Nobody drinks from the pool for seven days after a birth. We skim the pool, and the sun kills anything we can't see."

She wondered where she had been born. In the desert, somewhere.

"And you?" he asked, as if reading her thoughts. "Where did you come into the desert?"

She shook her head. "My mother didn't tell me."

"You didn't ask?"

She shrugged. "I never thought to." When her mother was killed one night, it had been too late for questions.

"I'm sorry," he said.

She looked at him, searching his dark eyes. He put a rough hand on her shoulder. "My mother, too," he said, "is dead. It is the natural process of life." He tilted his head towards the tree. "This tree lives, shelters us, gives us food, and one day it will also die." He smiled with one side of his mouth. "It doesn't make it any better, I know." He put his other hand over his heart. "The part of me where my mother was is still empty."

That emptiness was in her, too. She and her mother had known each other in a free, easy way. No arguments, and when there were arguments, they were quickly forgiven. They accepted each other without question. Other people were hard.

"Nobody knows you like your mother and the desert," he said. "That's what we say in the Garden. They both knew you before you knew yourself."

On the night her mother died, her screams—Murdergirl cut off the thoughts and looked away from Hux. Somehow, he made her think about things she thought she had left buried beneath the desert sand years ago.

"I'm sorry," he said again. "So," he cleared his throat, "I have seen Harissa with you a lot. A big change."

Murdergirl nodded and shrugged with a smile. "She likes me."

"More than that. I hear at first she was ready to let you die. But now she sees something in you."

She looked at him. "What do you think she sees?"

"I think everyone sees what they want to see." He stared out into the cloudless sky. "She sees hope."

"Hope." She laughed once. "And what do you see when you look at me?"

He turned towards her. Then his gaze moved down her body and back up to her face. His dark brown eyes searched hers. How long since she had simply looked at someone's eyes? And if he'd known what she was thinking even before, what might it be like if he was looking right into her eyes? Her heart beat faster.

"Nevermind," she said, suddenly looking away.

"I didn't mean—"

"No," she said, "it's alright. It's just that..." she sighed. "Back with the Bones, and before that even, in the desert, whose gaze could I meet?" She turned up one corner of her mouth. "Letting your guard down was inviting their knife into your ribs."

Through the thin palm slivers, she felt Hux's fingertips just on the edge of her hand. "It's not like that here," he said.

She pulled her hand away and stood up. "What about Harissa's mother?" she asked, changing the subject. "Where is she?"

Hux stayed seated. "Like a few others of us, Harissa mother left her in the Garden one night as a baby, while we were asleep, but we like to say that the desert brought her to us." He smiled. "Maybe there is some truth to it, because our guards were not alerted, and there were no footprints. Either way, like you, she came from the desert. Maybe that's why she did not like you at first, and also part of why she likes you now."

"It must have been hard for her, to find out she was left."

Hux tilted his head, considering. "I don't think so. The Garden is a good place, and her young life has had plenty of happiness and hard work. And because she never knew her mother, maybe she almost believes the story that the desert gave her to us."

Speaking of Harissa reminded Murdergirl of the river below the desert. "She showed me..." she trailed off. Maybe she wasn't supposed to have seen.

"The river," Hux said, finishing her sentence. "We gave her permission. It's okay for you to see the river. There is a ritual we do that is only for Gardeners, but anyone can see the river." He smiled. "Not that we would let Hambone in, for example, but in principle it's not forbidden for people to see it."

"Aren't I a Gardener?" she asked.

He shook his head. "Gardening doesn't make someone a Gardener."

"What does?"

"When you have it, you'll know."

She rolled her eyes. "Listening to you is like trying to read an old book."

"Nobody can read those anymore," he said.

"Exactly."

He smiled. When it was clear he wasn't going to say anything else, Murdergirl said, "Do you ever wonder what it would be like if the river was on top of the desert instead of down in the cave, so everybody could use it?"

"It would be crowded, I suppose. Like in the Garden, all the trees are around our stream, and all the tents are around that."

"I mean the whole river. Lots of it has to be undersand, not just what's in the cave. I've seen pictures of rivers from before, they go for a long way, farther than you can see. There would be enough room for everyone. If we could get everyone in the valley to work together..." she turned her palms up.

"Hambone, working with us? And nevermind the Bones, the Skinheads? They hardly care about anything, eating poison meat, killing others, killing themselves. Hand a Skinhead a bucket for water, and he will fill it with your blood." He stood up and leaned against the date palm. "I don't know about those old pictures."

"What do you mean?"

"I just don't know. I've seen some old pictures, too." He nodded towards the skeleton structures in the distance. "Pictures of that, some have said; full of people and machines, nobody hungry or angry. Nobody growing food either, so how did they eat?"

"Hear me. I don't know how they did it, but I know it." She turned her face away. "I've felt it."

"Felt it?"

Trying to explain the motorcycle would be like explaining the river to a crevice cricket. You had to feel the beast yourself.

"It doesn't matter," she said. "If the river was up here, things would be better. There would be enough for everybody."

"There already is enough. The desert gives us what we need."

"And then Hambone takes half."

Hux smiled. "You sound like Harissa. I, too, can imagine a world that is better. I can imagine we all work together. Don't I want that, too? So many have died before their time." He sighed and looked towards the mountains on the horizon with a furrowed brow. For a long moment, neither of them spoke. Only the breeze in the leaves made a sound. Then he looked back at her, his expression once again clear and smooth. "We do what we can. We have what we need."

Murdergirl leaned her back against the tree and looked down at the sand. It was hard to keep away the thoughts about the unfairness of the Bones taking what the Gardeners grew. But she couldn't stop the Bones. The two piles of greasewood bulbs caught her eye. The only thing to do about it was to work hard. She went to her knees and dug her hand into the sand. "Let's get back to work," she said, shifting her hand around, feeling for a prickly bulb.

Chapter 11

"Ready or not, here I come!" Murdergirl uncovered her eyes. She had a quick look around, though of course Harissa would not be hiding so close. Nearby, towards the rear of the camp, empty bamboo crates were piled one on top of another, some lying on their sides in the sand, and a nearby storage tent held crates bulging full with fruit, protected from the sun and insects by tightly woven seals. They had harvested most of the fruit of the main growing season, and drying had already started.

She adjusted her headscarf. Harissa spent a lot of time in Murdergirl's tent when she wasn't in there, that might be where the girl was hiding. But going in through the front would be too easy, especially when she could crawl through the loose flap at the back. She smiled and stifled a laugh, imagining how surprised Harissa would be.

Harissa was now right on the edge of womanhood; another year, even another six months, would she have any interest in games? Yet, she had picked up the game quickly; although Murdergirl was a master, having played it with her mother for years in caves and among dunes and rusted wrecks. There was something important in games. Something that took you away from the world for a moment, that let a child just be a child. The Bones drank their wine and shouted and fought for the same reason, maybe the Skinheads even killed for the same reason.

Murdergirl went through the piled crates to circle around to the rear of her tent. A familiar shape, draped in white, stopped her. She hadn't thought of it for weeks. The motorcycle stood, motionless; the beast was sleeping. She felt the shape of the handles, and even through the canvas she could feel the beast's power. She slipped the cover off, and her breath caught in her throat as the canvas revealed the beast's shining chrome and polished leather. It was magnificent. Riding this, shotgun in hand, nobody could stop you, nobody could catch you. It all came back. The desert raced away beneath her, and mountains grew in the distance. She could feel the wind against her face and whipping through her hair as it flowed out behind her, needle climbing to four-zero, five-zero, six-zero. Turns sprayed sand into the air. The shotgun pressed cold between her shoulders. Her hand moved on its own, as if to wake the beast. She stopped and looked down. Her thumb and forefinger gripped tight on the metal, knuckles white. She blinked. She wasn't racing through the desert; she was standing in the Garden. Slowly, she pulled her hand back. She held that hand in her other and looked at it. There was a power in the beast, more than just its raw mechanical power. There was something in it that made you want it.

"Gotcha!" Small fingers dug into her ribs, and Murdergirl jumped, whirling around to see Harissa's grinning face.

"I've been waiting for*ever*," Harissa said.

"Sorry," Murdergirl said. "I was looking. I…" she glanced back at the motorcycle.

"Wow." Harissa poked her head around Murdergirl. "Is that the beast?"

"That's what I call it. The people who made it called them motorcycles."

"Does it bite?"

Murdergirl smiled. "It's not that kind of beast. It's a machine. It stays asleep unless you give it power."

"Can I touch it?" She asked, already reaching her hand out. Murdergirl nodded, and Harissa put her hands on the motorcycle. First the leather seat, then the chrome body, then the rubber handles. "It's so weird," she said. Then, "What does it do when you give it power?"

"Well, it wakes up." She'd told Harissa all of this before. "It growls. If you give it more power, it roars. And you can ride it, it takes you anywhere, fast."

"Like the skin horses?"

"Like that. But it doesn't get tired. And it's faster, so much faster. Riding the beast is like riding a sandstorm."

Harissa looked at Murdergirl, and her pale, aloe-oiled face lit with a smile. "Take me on it."

"What?"

"Come on, let's ride it." She slapped the leather seat. "You control it. There's room for both of us."

Murdergirl's heart beat faster. There was nothing more she wanted than to get on the beast and ride. Nothing else was the same as the feeling of squeezing your thighs against all that power. And she wanted to share it with Harissa, to share it with everyone, even. But there was something else she wanted, even if she didn't know what, that's why she had pulled her hand back from the metal before. She shook her head.

Harissa stood on tiptoes and looked over the bamboo crates. "Nobody is there, you won't get in trouble if you take me."

"It's not that," Murdergirl said. "It's just... it's dangerous."

"Dangerous?" Harissa scoffed. "Come on, Murdergirl! I just want one ride. I took you to the river. I Watered you even when they said not to!"

"Harissa!"

"Not you too," Harissa moaned. "I wanted to share it with you. I thought we were friends."

"We are friends."

"Then why won't you show me yours?"

"What you have here, the Garden, it's good. It's yours. It's better than any machine could be. Don't you understand?"

Harissa rolled her eyes. "Look, if you don't want to share it with me, just say so. Don't make up some stupid thing."

"But I—"

Harissa held up her hand and pressed her lips together, her eyes shiny with tears. Then she turned and ran, kicking a crate as she went.

Murdergirl watched her go. She looked down at the motorcycle and sighed, then pulled the canvas back over it. She righted the crate Harissa had kicked over. Even without power, it seemed the beast was still dangerous. When Harissa had Watered her, she had asked if Murdergirl wanted to be part of the Garden. She did want that. Even as exciting as it was to ride the beast, when you rode, you rode alone. In the Garden, she had everyone, and everyone had her. Harissa had never been alone, had always had the Garden, and did not know what it might mean to go away from that, and even how the beast might pull her away or put her in danger.

“She is young,” Rebecca said. “Emotions are highest when you are young.”

“You know that I was born of the desert,” Murdergirl said. “Out there, there were only hyenas and lizards to please, and a rock usually pleased them both the same.”

“Your mother?”

“We lived so close. It was like having one mind. If she was upset, I knew why, I knew how to fix it. But with Harissa? She clearly has her own mind, and it’s not shared. She won’t even speak to me, she hasn’t for two days.”

Rebecca smiled. “Yes, she has her own mind.” The old woman held out a piece of purple fruit. “Fig?”

“No, thanks.” At the end of the year’s major harvest, the Garden clearly had an excess of fruit, and people constantly offered food to each other. “In the desert, my body almost learned not to eat food.”

Rebecca popped the fruit into her mouth and chewed, the seeds crunching loudly. “In the Garden, learning to eat food is a lifelong lesson.” She held out another fig.

Murdergirl took the fruit. To be a Gardener, she would have to eat like one. She bit into the fig’s chewy flesh. For a few moments, the only sound other than the loud night chirping of the crevice crickets was the chewing and crunching of figs.

Rebecca gestured towards the outside of the camp with a half-eaten fig. “These torches we keep around the Garden at night.”

“To keep hyenas away?”

Rebecca nodded. “Hyenas, cripple snakes, Skinheads—though what’s the difference there, I don’t know—all the bad things, they stay away from the light. You know where we get the torches?"

"From the Forge."

Rebecca nodded. "Our bamboo flames, but too quickly and too noisily for a torch. Like anything else to do with flame, the Forge knows best." She took a bite of fig. "Have you been to the Forge?"

Murdergirl shook her head. She had only seen the red glow of the Forge from a distance.

"They will only let you in at night, so we trade with them at night." The old woman paused, pulling seeds out of her teeth with her tongue. "I want you to go."

"Me? Representing the garden?"

Rebecca nodded. "Take Harissa with you."

"She won't go."

"We survive by feeding the Garden, and the Garden feeds us. Every Gardener knows that. The Garden needs torches. She will go."

Murdergirl slung the sack onto her back. It was heavy, full of dried fruit, enough to last one person for several weeks if they restrained themselves. Hux helped her secure the straps. His slender fingers lingered for a moment on her upper arms.

"Harissa knows the way," he said, "and no hyena will come near a torch."

"Thank you."

"Watch where you step. Death by the sting of a cripple snake is painful and long."

"Hux." She looked at him. "I've lived in the desert longer than you. I am not going to be stung by a cripple snake."

He smiled. "I know. Especially not when you have our Harissa with you. Right, Harissa?"

"Let's go," Harissa said. She set off into the desert, immediately fading into the night.

Good luck, Hux mouthed, with smiling eyes.

Murdergirl pulled her torch out of the sand and followed Harissa. The girl walked in darkness, only lit from behind by Murdergirl's torch.

"How far is it?" Murdergirl asked, after they had been walking for a few minutes.

No response. Murdergirl blew out her breath. Marching for who knows how long in the night desert with a grumpy guide was not how she'd wanted to spend tonight. It had to be a long distance, because they could not see the light of the Forge. With no conversation, she would have to focus on her work. Maybe it would be better—talking could distract you from the approaching paws of a hyena. The torch, while casting a very clear circle of light around her, also blinded her eyes to the darkness beyond, making her ears her primary tool. The soft crunch of their own feet in the sand. Crevice crickets and their constant nighttime song. The torch, crackling. Crunch, crickets, crackling. Crunch, crickets, crackling. And that, was it the far-away laughter of a hyena? Her ears strained to hear. It stopped.

"Did you hear that?" she asked.

No response. Harissa did not slow her pace, did not move her head.

"Even if I wanted to take you for a ride, we can't. Hambone thinks I'm dead and the motorcycle is lost to the desert. If he hears its roar, he'll come for it, and he'll come for me. He'll come to the Garden."

Still nothing from Harissa.

"Okay," Murdergirl said, "I guess it's just me out here. I hope I don't get attacked by a pack of hyenas." She swayed her torch side to side, making Harissa's shadow leap nimbly back and forth. "Just me, all on my own out here in the desert." She cleared her throat loudly. "You hear that?" she called out. "Just me out in the desert, just like it used to be. No point being with anybody else or even talking to another person, they only hurt you."

In the distance, was that the rhythmic thud of hooves? It too died away. Only people with bad intentions rode skin horses. Skinheads would skin you, that was clear from the corpses she'd seen with the skin removed from their skulls. People said they'd eat you too, like they ate the meat of their poisonous cattle.

The torch made them a target. In the dark, you could see it miles away. Animals would not come close, but the wrong kind of humans might. It was a necessary risk, because without the torch, Hux's cripple snake would slither right under your foot, and a hyena would tear your throat out to drink your blood.

"Yes," she said, "I sure don't want to get attacked by a hyena. If one of them ripped me to pieces and chewed on my insides, I don't know what I'd do." She began to whistle a short, sharp, repeated chirp, like a pocket mouse searching for food.

"Will you shut up?" Harissa said.

"Oh!" Murdergirl cried in mock surprise. "I didn't see you there. I thought I was alone here. Just me and my crickets. And a pocket mouse, I think. My apologies, Miss."

"You're going to get us actually killed by drawing attention."

"Anybody out there can see us anyway," Murdergirl said. She waved the torch, making Harissa's shadow dance again.

"Yes, and now they can hear us. They know you're a woman. And if that wasn't bad enough, they also know you're an idiot."

"It's not—"

"What if the Bones are out there? What if they recognize your voice? You think a torch is going to keep them away?"

"I get it," Murdergirl said. "If you don't want me talking to myself, then you talk to me."

"Why should I? You don't even care about me."

"That's ridiculous," she said to the back of the girl's head. "I've been spending tons of time with you, doing everything with you."

"But the thing that's really important, that you really like, your motorcycle, you won't share it with me."

"It's not about sharing," Murdergirl protested. "I want to share, but I'm trying to protect you."

"It is about sharing! Everything is. Gardeners share, we share everything. We share with each other as—"

"As the desert shares with us?" Murdergirl finished. "I know, but this is still different. And as everybody always tells me, I'm not a Gardener anyway."

Harissa spun around. "You think you're not a Gardener?" The flames burned in her eyes.

"Do you… think I am?"

"What do you think I Watered you for?" Harissa shouted. "They told me not to, and I did it. I made you a Gardener."

For a moment, Murdergirl did not know what to say. She looked at Harissa's set jaw. Then she said, "Turn around, you're going to mess up your eyes."

Harissa scoffed. "That's it?"

"I didn't realize you thought I was a Gardener."

"You are!"

"Sorry, look, okay. I didn't realize I was a Gardener. Hux said I didn't have the thing in me that makes me one."

"They all say stuff like that," Harissa said. "You garden. You've been Watered. You're a Gardener."

When she put it like that, it was hard not to agree. And Rebecca had sent her out on a fairly dangerous mission, would she do that with an outsider?

"Okay. So I am a Gardener. There are still some things that can't be shared. I went on the motorcycle. Yes, it's amazing. Then I almost died. When you found me, Rebecca said I was cooked like a cactus nut. If the desert had kept me a little longer, then there would be nothing to share. No words, no stories, no games, no fun, no midnight hikes in the desert to get torches. Now will you please turn around?"

Harissa huffed, turned to face the darkness, and walked into it again.

"Look, I'm sorry," Murdergirl said. "I'm not trying to hurt you. It's only because you're important to me. I don't want you to have the life I've had. It's hard. It's cruel. I've done things I don't even want to think about. I've had to be a bad person."

Harissa didn't respond. Murdergirl sighed. Probably better without talking anyway, she could focus on the sounds out in the darkness. Back to just the crunching of their feet in the sand again.

But it wasn't just the crunching. Something else was out there. She strained her ears. Almost like footsteps, but heavier. Faster. "Stop," she whispered to Harissa.

"Murdergirl—"

"*Hush,*" Murdergirl hissed. They both stopped. The sounds stopped at the same time. Harissa, sensing the urgency in Murdergirl's voice, dropped to a knee and peered into the darkness. As Murdergirl's ears adjusted to the quiet, she could hear breathing; her own, Harissa's—and more.

Out of the darkness something whistled through the air and smashed into Harissa's face. Blood sprayed into the air, glittering in the torchlight. The girl grunted and collapsed back against Murdergirl. Murdergirl dropped to her knees, letting Harissa slide down to the ground. The rough wooden club that had hit Harissa lay in the sand, one end slicked with her blood.

"Who's out there?" Murdergirl called. She turned back and forth, waving the torch. Whoever it was, they didn't want to come close to the torch, and she couldn't see anything beyond the circle of light. Harissa wasn't moving; her red hair lay over her bloody red face. Murdergirl knelt beside her, put her hand on the girl's face—she was breathing.

More noise in the darkness. Heavy footsteps. Not steps. *Hooves.* She slowed her breathing. Had to move fast, but carefully. Plan it. One chance. How many hooves? Maybe two sets. She listened for a moment. Both of them there, right in front. She shrugged her arms out of the sack on her back; she needed to move quickly.

She hurled the torch forward. As it whirled crazily through the night, it lit two skin horses, patches of gray hair over red, festering flesh, and their riders—Skinheads, their faces grotesque masks of dried blood and matted hair. Only about ten strides away. The torch landed a horse-length past the Skinheads and silhouetted them, its flame sputtering against the sand. Murdergirl pulled the shotgun off her back, where it had rested beneath the sack of fruit. She brought the sight up and fired. The shot exploded into the night, and one Skinhead dropped from his horse, leaking blood from a dozen holes. She turned it on the other and fired, just as his horse bolted. Some of the shot hit him, but most missed, and he landed on his feet.

The torch flame dimmed. The shotgun was empty. She reached for the bag of shells at her waist, but her hand found nothing. Fuck. It had fallen off. Even wounded, the Skinhead was still strong. He wore only a dirty loincloth, and his firmly muscled body shone in the flickering flame, slick with blood and sweat.

She flipped the shotgun around, holding the barrel in both hands, ready to swing. The Skinhead picked up the throwing club his dead partner had dropped. The flame fizzled and dimmed further. Through the mask of skin and hair, the Skinhead's mouth formed a smile and showed his teeth. Skinheads were used to the darkness; when the flame went, he would have them. Her hands gripped tightly on the gun; her muscles strained. Only a spot of light from the flame remained. He stepped towards them and raised his weapon.

Fuck this. She was going to smash his skull or die trying. She ran at him, screaming.

A monstrous hyena sprang from the blackness onto the Skinhead. Only a few steps away, Murdergirl stopped, skidded in the sand, and fell on her ass. The hyena bit down on the Skinhead's shoulder and he screamed as his bones cracked. Murdergirl scrambled backwards to Harissa. Another hyena joined the first and bit into the Skinhead's leg. The flame died.

Chapter 12

Murdergirl bumped into Harissa's body, and the girl moaned. She put out her hands, feeling Harissa's face; they came away wet with blood. "We have to go," Murdergirl said. Harissa groaned in response. "Come on, we have to go *now*." She put her hands under Harissa's armpits and hauled the girl to her feet, then pulled one of Harissa's arms over her own shoulders. "Let's go," she said. "One foot in front of the other." Harissa sagged. Murdergirl walked, dragging Harissa beside her. She couldn't carry her. She let Harissa down and sank to her knees.

"Harissa, hear this. There are hyenas just a few steps away." In the moonlight, she saw Harissa's eyes open.

"Hyenas?"

The Skinhead screamed in response.

"Yes. If we don't get out of here, the next scream is going to be yours. Can you stand?"

"I... I think so," the girl said. "I'll try." Murdergirl tugged under Harissa's armpits again, and they stood up together.

"Oh, my head." Moonlight reflected off Harissa's teeth as she grimaced.

"Don't worry about your head. Worry about your legs."

The hyenas growled and snapped at each other, fighting over the best parts of the Skinhead.

Harissa took a step forward and Murdergirl felt her wobble. She pulled the girl close to her with one arm around her. "I've got you," she whispered. They walked together as one, with shuffling steps, facing away from the hyenas and the Skinhead. The hair on the back of Murdergirl's neck stood up—it was hard to turn away from those vicious creatures. The Skinhead's screams had quieted now, replaced by pitiful moans as his blood poured from his body and his strength with it. Harissa kept her face pressed against Murdergirl, as if hiding the sight that she couldn't see anyway in the darkness. Every few seconds there was the sickly sound of flesh tearing as the hyenas ripped chunks from the Skinhead's flesh. And as they ate, they laughed, chuckling through the meat and blood while he was still alive. They had chosen him instead of the one already dead. Murdergirl fought to keep her stomach settled, but her gorge rose, and vomit spewed onto the sand. She would have given anything for a torch, anything so they didn't have to walk completely exposed and defenseless, aware that at any moment those monsters could leap onto them, and it could be their blood spraying out into the desert while the hyenas laughed and ate. But there was nothing. She sidestepped where she had been sick and they kept walking.

As they walked, the ground changed. It was hard underfoot, and easier to walk on. Not sand anymore. The sounds of the hyenas' grisly meal faded into the distance. Murdergirl's eyes had now adjusted to the darkness, and the moon gave just enough light to see the shape of the land. Rock formations rose around them, and she had to pay more attention to where she put their feet. Hopefully this was the right way to go. Harissa could not guide them. Even if it was wrong, putting more distance between them and the hyenas could only be a good thing. A huge rock, dozens of strides wide and more, and just as tall, blocked their path;

Murdergirl took them around it, gently guiding Harissa beside her. As they rounded the side of the rock, far ahead, a faint red glow lit the sky. Relaxation was impossible, but some of the tension went from Murdergirl's shoulders. She looked down at Harissa, who seemed to be walking with her eyes closed.

"Hey," she said, "look."

Harissa raised her head away from Murdergirl's shoulder and looked. For a long moment, she said nothing. Tears streaked down her bloody cheeks. "We're going to make it," she said.

Every step drew them closer to the blood-red glow. Ahead, rock slabs as sharp as daggers and taller than ten people jutted up from the ground, painted crimson by the light. The ground was dry, hard-packed clay, veined with a network of cracks. Rocks littered the landscape in all directions, from small ankle-breakers to enormous boulders larger than the whole Garden. Gradually, the ground became more rock than soil, until they were walking entirely on a plateau of rock. Bits of ash coated the rock, thinner and more delicate underfoot even than the papers of the centuries-old books the Bones used for flame.

"I think I'm okay to walk now," Harissa said. She stopped and faced Murdergirl. "How do I look?"

Blood smeared her face, and it was thick and crusted around the gash on her forehead. Some hair stuck to her skin, glued by blood, and matted hair soaked in blood framed her face. Murdergirl's face must have shown what it looked like, and Harissa burst out laughing, causing the dried blood around her mouth and eyes to crack.

"Let's just say you've looked better," Murdergirl said. "I'll wash you."

She reached for the sack on her back, but her hand came back with nothing. She'd taken it off when the Skinheads attacked. It hadn't just held fruit, but also their water. Suddenly her mouth felt dry. They wouldn't thirst to death, but it was a long walk back to the Garden.

"Looking for this?" Harissa held up the sack.

"How did you..."

The girl shrugged. "I guess I picked it up."

"And you've been carrying it this whole time, when you could barely walk? Why didn't you say something?"

"Why don't *you* say something, something like 'nice work'?"

"Right. Sorry." Murdergirl smiled. She returned the sack to her back. "Good work. It's no wonder you could barely walk though, carrying both. I thought you were actually hurt."

Harissa playfully shoved Murdergirl. "I *am* hurt!" She pointed to her forehead.

"That's just a scratch." Murdergirl took the sack and pulled out a bottle of water. They each took a long drink, and then she washed the blood from Harissa's face.

The landscape of rocks around them drew in closer, leading them towards what looked like an entrance—two huge rock slabs, crossed in an 'X' shape.

"Stop," a voice commanded. A man wearing a heavy leather apron stepped through the entrance and blocked their path. Besides the apron, he only wore a thin leather strap around his groin. He held a thick wooden spear and had the muscles to show he could hurl it straight through any body he chose. "What are you here for?" he demanded.

"Shamon, it's me," Harissa said.

"I'm talking to her," he said, pointing his spear at Murdergirl. "Why does a Bone come to the Forge, after what Hambone has done?"

"I'm not a Bone anymore," Murdergirl said. She reached for the sack on her back, and Shamon took a step forward, with both hands on his spear. She took her hand away and held up her open palms. "I'll go slow," she said. Very carefully, she slipped the straps off her back. She pulled open the mouth of the sack to show the dried fruit inside. "Rebecca sent me."

"She's a Gardener now," Harissa said.

"A Gardener? She has been watered?"

"Yep." Harissa grinned. "I watered her myself."

"What happened to your head?" he asked Harissa.

"Skinheads," Murdergirl said.

"They are harsh visitors indeed, no matter where or when."

"Murdergirl saved me," Harissa said.

"Murdergirl? You have kept your Bones name?"

She nodded. "It's the only name I have now."

"Whatever her name, she killed both Skinheads," Harissa said. "She's with me, and we're here to trade."

Shamon rested the base of his spear on the ground. "In that case, little one, what are you trading for?"

"Same as always," Harissa said. "More torches."

Shamon looked back and forth between them. "You came without a torch?"

"Lost in the fight," Murdergirl said.

"Then you are certainly in need." He stepped closer to them. "But first," he said, taking the shotgun off Murdergirl's back, "you must leave this with me. The heart of the desert forbids such things inside the Forge." She let him take it without protest—it was empty anyway, extra shells were all the way back at the Garden. He turned and walked through the rock archway, gesturing with his spear for them to follow.

They came into a roughly circular area about two hundred paces across, a natural arena. The center was hard, cracked clay. Around that the ground turned to stone again, rising here and there in gradual, natural steps, until at the edge of the circle it formed a high stone wall. At several points around the edge, crumbling pillars stood. Were they natural formations, or from the time before? Several Forge-mates were dotted around the upper rim of the wall between the pillars, keeping watch into the valley beyond.

"With the height advantage of the wall," Shamon said to Murdergirl, "we can see anyone long before they arrive. And with only one entrance, even just two or three of us could hold against thirty. Even the old ones with their tall buildings would have been impressed by what the desert has made for us."

Here and there in the stone there were natural caves. Forge-mates drifted in and out of them. A few of the caves were man made, gouged out, their walls covered in tool marks; these were not large, and the back wall of each of them could clearly be seen. Several caves had a few people near the entrance, clustered around barrels filled with flame. From time to time, a Forge-mate poured liquid flame into a barrel. Other caves breathed black smoke from their mouths.

To one side of the stone arena, a path opened and the stone rose up towards what would have been called a mountain if not for the mountains all around the valley that dwarfed it. Red-black smoke poured out from the peak. For

Murdergirl's whole life, it had lit one end of the Valley's sky with a reddish glow.

"What is it?" Murdergirl asked, pointing.

"A volcano," Shamon said. "The burning heart of the desert." He led them away from the path into one of the caves.

"Is Pig here?" Harissa asked.

"As always," he replied.

The cave entrance tunnel was dark, but a few steps in they rounded a corner and it was lit by torches. It was warm inside the cave. Further in, it became warmer. Then it was hot, and with every step it became hotter. Sweat rolled from Murdergirl's forehead. The path sloped downwards, and they walked down into the heat.

The cave opened up. It was lit with the same glow that came from the top of the volcano, but in the cave it dazzled the eyes. The heat that had built as they walked through the tunnel now reached a peak, hotter than the noon sun in the desert. Hot air dried Murdergirl's throat and made her lungs ache. A pool of a thick reddish-yellow liquid sat in the center of the cave, with a circle of smooth rock around it, and a stone trough leading a rivulet through an opening in the cave wall. Another Forge-mate stood in the cave, facing the pool but from a distance, the thick, black hair on his back nearly like a fur robe. He was tall, at least a head taller than Murdergirl.

"It's lava," Harissa whispered to Murdergirl. "Melted rock."

It was beautiful. And dangerous. Murdergirl could sense that the heat in the room radiated from the lava; the heat must be incredible to melt rock itself.

The Forge-mate turned. He removed a pair of heavily scratched sunglasses from the time before. "It rises from the center of the desert," he said. "From its burning heart."

"Pig!" Harissa ran and threw her arms around him. The hair that sprouted on his chest at the top of his apron met the hair on Harissa's head.

"They've come from the Garden to trade," Shamon said. He gestured to Murdergirl. "And this is Murdergirl."

"Murdergirl?" Pig furrowed his brow. "Well, a friend to this little one is a friend to me." He turned to Harissa. "So, let me guess, you've come for torches?" he asked. A smile shone out from the dark, wiry beard that reached his chest. "Just once, I hope that someone will come just to talk with old Pig, to seek my knowledge!" He wiped his eyes in mock sadness. "But until then," he tipped his head back, eyes closed, and spread his arms out. "I am but a lowly smith, a Forge-mate, doomed to drudgery and despair." He opened his eyes a bit, head still tilted back, and looked at Harissa, who was staring at him impassively. "Ah, is there no sympathy for Pig in this cruel world!"

Harissa punched him lightly in the stomach.

"You know," Pig said to Murdergirl, "I've known this girl since she was a wee baby, barely bigger than a pocket mouse. I carried her in my own pocket, you know, like a kangaroo."

"You did not!" Harissa said. "What's a kangaroo?"

"Kangaroo?" Pig asked with a grin, as if he could not believe any person did not know what a kangaroo was. "Big creature. Teeth as big as your nose. Legs for days, could kick your head clean off."

Harissa rolled her eyes, trying to suppress her own smile. "Quit making things up. How about some torches?"

"Torches, oh, torches again!" He pulled down the corners of his mouth into a huge frown. "I am ill-used and ill-treated, and by this pocket mouse of a girl, no less." He led them to an opening at the side of the cave. "How the mighty have fallen."

They went down several rough-cut stone steps into a small cave. It was much cooler in there, lower down and away from the lava. Murdergirl took a deep breath of the cool air. Inside this cave there were bundles of torches, some as thin as a finger and others as thick as a leg, with the upper portion of each wrapped in fibrous strips and coated with a glossy black substance. Murdergirl and Harissa handed over their sacks of fruit. Pig picked up two large bundles, each with more than fifty of the thin torches.

"Don't you want to check the sacks?" Murdergirl asked.

"No need," Pig said. "The Garden and the Forge would not cheat each other. If either did, both would suffer, and nothing would be gained." He motioned them back towards the main cave. "Come, don't you find it's a bit too cold away from our warm friend the lava?"

Murdergirl took one last breath of the cool air and they ascended. The air grew hotter. Even with previous exposure to the oppressive heat, her lungs protested with each breath. Pig must have noticed something in her expression, because he asked, "It's not too hot for you, is it?"

"No... it's just... yes." She blinked as sweat stung her eyes. "It's like what they say happened at the end of the before, when God opened up a lake of flame for Satan."

"Pig says he was born in here," Harissa said.

"Aye," Pig said. "Born and raised by the volcano, and the burning heart of the desert beats in my own chest." Even so, sweat beaded on his forehead, too. "Don't forget to light a torch before you go," he said, "for the journey back." He gently placed his hand over Harissa's forehead. "I don't like you going into the desert with Skinheads about."

"I'm not a little girl anymore, Pig."

"I know. I know. But to me, you'll always be the little one I carried in my pocket."

"You didn't carry me in your pocket!"

Pig smiled. "Like a kangaroo."

"Is there anything you can give us to help?" Murdergirl said.

Pig looked at her for a moment. "Only Forge-mates..." he trailed off. "Follow me." He led them along the stone trough that carried a stream of the lava into another opening in the wall. Inside, the lava collected in a small pool, only a foot or two across. Murdergirl stood right next to it; it was still hot, but much more bearable than the large pool in the main cave. A tangle of ancient bicycles laid on the ground. Most had no wheels, and of those that did, the tires had rotted away long before and the remaining metal was bent into crazy shapes.

"There's no riding these anymore," Pig said, "but the heart of the desert doesn't just melt stone." He put on rough-sewn leather mitts and picked up a y-shaped piece of a bicycle frame. He held the joint of the frame in the lava for several seconds. When he removed it, the lava fell away, and the metal glowed white-hot. In his other hand, he picked up a large rock. He placed the hot metal on the edge of the pool and bashed the rock against it, creating a *clang* that resounded in the small space and Murdergirl felt in her bones. He bashed it again, and part of the frame fell away into the lava. It floated for a moment, then sank below the surface. In his hand, Pig now held one long, straight section of metal from the bicycle. He dipped the tip into the lava again and took it out, then hit the rock against the metal again and again. The metal cooled as he smashed it. He held it up, the red tip now formed into a point.

"It's like a spear," Harissa said.

Pig nodded. "But the spears we make from Oasis trees don't throw true, and they easily splinter." He tossed the bicycle spear into the air and easily caught it in his hand again.

Murdergirl's eyes moved over the pile of bicycles. "You could make hundreds of these," she said.

Pig raised his bushy eyebrows. "I suppose we could. But there are only a few of us Forge-mates, and the others would not use these."

Light and silent. Easy to carry. The point of the bicycle spear Pig held would go right through the skull of a Skinhead. Or Hambone…

Harissa looked up at her. "What are you thinking?"

"Nothing." Murdergirl shook her head. "Is that for us?" she asked Pig.

Harissa reached out, but Pig pulled it away. "Not this one. Too hot. It will be hours before it cools." He went to the pile of bicycles and pulled out a couple of short spears, each about an arm long, and passed them over. "I made these earlier."

Murdergirl slowly waved her spear through the air. It was even lighter than she'd thought. She tossed it up and caught it again.

"It's hollow inside," Pig said. "So, it's light, but the metal is still very strong. It's amazing. I don't know how they made this in the time before. If only I knew the technique…"

"Are you doing more things like this?" Murdergirl asked.

He shrugged. "Some things. The others in the Forge wouldn't want me to talk about it with you. They don't like me doing it at all." He frowned behind his beard. "But if we only knew."

"If the rest of the Forge-mates helped, if you were all working towards the same goal..." she sighed in frustration. "Hear this, Pig. Don't you feel it? The past? The whole machine that they built in the time before? And now we live in caves, like animals. You could talk to the others. They would listen to you!"

"It can't happen," he said. "It is not the Forge way."

"The Gardeners could help," Harissa said.

Pig smiled. "Talking about it will only waste our breath. How many years have you been visiting the Forge, little one?"

"Fifteen years? All my life."

He nodded. "Then you know why people live like they do now..." he looked at Murdergirl and his smile went away, "...like animals. The people before angered the whole world, and it pushed us away, it poisoned everything except our valley, so that we live here, simply, and cannot go to raise the giant machine skeletons from before. There are ways to live that are good, with flame and stone and wood and plants, and ways that are bad."

"If that's true," Murdergirl said, "if you really believe that, then why are you making these bicycle spears? Why do you want the technique to make their hollow metal? Don't you truly want us, Forge-mates and Gardeners all, working together to rediscover the past, to make our own future, to push away the Bones and the Skinheads?"

Pig looked down at the bicycle spear he had made, its tip still red-hot.

"You're right," he said. "The Skinheads especially are terrible. But they are on their farm, and they stay there." He glanced at the wound on Harissa's forehead and grimaced. "Mostly, they stay there. And so we leave them where they are. That pull you speak of, it's in every human. Meddle with people who are not your own. Build things you cannot control. Impossible to avoid the pull completely." He opened his hand and let the spear fall. It clattered on the stone floor. "But we do our best."

Chapter 13

The torch crackled behind Murdergirl. On the journey back, she was to be their eyes into the darkness. She walked several strides in front of Harissa, and the torch only illuminated the sand a few steps ahead. She could see the lines of the land around and in the distance, and she would see any shapes that moved, but directly ahead it was like stepping towards the edge of a cliff that hung over a black abyss. Still, she walked, trusting the desert.

"I hope you're not mad at Pig," Harissa said.

"Not mad," she replied. She thought for a moment, listening to the *crunch, crunch* of their feet. What to say? Harissa's life with the Garden was wonderful, though she could not see it because it was the only way she had ever lived. She could not turn the girl against their ways.

"What, then?"

Murdergirl sighed. There was no avoiding an issue when you were walking for miles in near pitch-darkness and had to stay close to the only other person who also happened to be holding the torch.

"You know the ruined old buildings we can see the tops of," Murdergirl asked, "beyond the mountains?"

"Of course."

"Do you ever wonder what it would be like in those buildings, to be at the top, looking out at the world? From there, you could see the desert. Everything would be below you. Even the volcano at the Forge would be small."

"I do wonder that, sometimes," Harissa said. "But we can't go there. It's dangerous. Even the Skinheads don't leave the valley."

"What if we made our own, here? Our own city. We could be high in a tower, safe from Bones and Skinheads. We would have more than enough food and water for everyone. Lectric lights would keep the hyenas and cripple snakes away."

Harissa laughed. "Lectric lights? Come on, you're as bad as Pig! Lectricity is just a story old people tell kids. Even I tell the little ones about it myself now."

Murdergirl suddenly felt cold. She stopped and turned around to face Harissa. "It's not just a story," Murdergirl said. Was everything from the time before going to be lost, were they going to lose more and more, until they truly did become like animals, scrabbling in the sand for grubs and greasewood and never knowing that they could be more?

"What are you talking about?"

"I've seen lectric lights. The place where I got the shotgun and the motorcycle beast, it has them."

Harissa smiled for a second and it went away just as quickly. "Are you serious?"

"I am."

"Because it isn't funny if you're not."

"Harissa, I'm not lying. There are, in this desert, still lectric lights."

The girl's smile came back, big and bright in the light from the flame. "Take me to it."

Murdergirl opened her mouth to say no automatically, but stopped. Harissa needed to see it, just like she had. It had changed her. That's when she had realized they could be more and do more, when she had stumbled on that bunker by chance. Living a life of just sand makes you an expert on sand, but there could be more to life than sand. "Okay," she said.

"Woo!" Harissa shouted. "You promise?"

Murdergirl smiled. "I promise. Keep quiet. You don't want to bring a hyena here, do you?"

"I laugh at hyenas," Harissa said.

"Oh, you do, do you?"

"Sure." Harissa slid a bicycle spear out of the bundle of torches on her back, where she had hidden it. She swished it around. "And when they start laughing, I just..." she jabbed the air repeatedly with the sharp, metal spear. "Right in the neck." With a final jab, Harissa returned the bicycle spear to the torch bundle. "What's it like there?"

"It's..." How to describe it? "It's safe. The walls, floor, and ceiling, they're solid, like stone, and as flat and smooth as your palm. And the walls are so thick you can't even hear the wind, like being in the Garden's cave but without the river. It's cool in the day, and warm during the night. The lectric lights stay on all the time, you never have to light them, and they don't flicker like flame. It's like the sun right there with you. There are all kinds of things from the old times, but they aren't broken, not like the bikes Pig has or the ships in the Valley. Everything is shiny, new, just like when they first made it."

"Will you take me there on the motorcycle?"

Murdergirl laughed and looked up at the stars. So they weren't past that after all.

"I won't be mad if you say no," Harissa said. "But I do really want to ride it."

Who wouldn't? She'd said it herself, riding that metal beast was like riding the power of a sandstorm. And if you went fast enough, it was like you had wings.

"Alright," she said. "I hear you. If." She raised her finger, stopping Harissa who was ready to shout again. "If Rebecca says that it's okay, I'll take you to the bunker on the motorcycle."

Harissa thought for a moment and then nodded her head. "Okay."

"So," Murdergirl said, pointing over her shoulder with her thumb, "can we go back to the Garden now?"

"Let's go," Harissa said. "So, you're definitely not mad at Pig?"

Murdergirl started walking again and shrugged. "He still gave us the spears, didn't he? I don't think he feels the same as the other Forge-mates. Maybe he shouldn't be at the Forge." If he could help. Perhaps Hux, perhaps Pig. How many others could see the world that was right at their fingertips?

"Maybe," Harissa said. "But they're all his friends. He's lived with them a long time, maybe his whole life."

Friends. She supposed Harissa was her friend. Rebecca, and Hux, too. A few of the others in the Garden. But how long had they known each other, a couple of months? And the Garden was a pleasant place, friendly people, hard work and good rewards, but would it last? She stared into the darkness as she walked. Her mother had been her only friend, the only relationship she'd ever had where they truly knew each other. Would she have ever given that up if it hadn't been taken from her?

Distant hoofbeats pulled Murdergirl out of her thoughts.

"Murdergirl, do you hear that?"

She stopped walking and held up her hand for silence. The sound faded away.

"It's safe," she said, and continued walking.

"Is it Skinheads?" Harissa asked.

"Nobody else would take the risk of riding those diseased animals. You know, for so long I've been thinking of the Bones as the problem in the valley."

"They are," Harissa said.

"Yes, but compared to a Skinhead? You know where you stand with a Bone. A Skinhead… a Skinhead is like an animal. Like a hyena. With them in the valley, we can never be safe."

"You just said we were safe," Harissa said.

"Yes, but…" Murdergirl paused a moment. Then she saw the tiny circles of flamelight that marked the perimeter of the Garden far ahead. "But we're close now, look." She pointed them out.

"Finally," Harissa said. "Tonight has been too long!"

Murdergirl nodded. Some of the tension went out of her muscles. It had been a long journey. Discussion of the Skinheads could wait.

Two torches broke away from the Garden and came towards them, orbs of light in the darkness. Murdergirl looked back at Harissa and they shared a frown. The next few minutes stretched into infinity; all they could do was continue to put one foot in front of the other as their flame gradually drew closer to the other two. Why would Gardeners come to meet them? What could be so important that it wouldn't wait a few more minutes? Something inside her yearned for more shotgun shells; she was never going out with a bag of shells tied so loosely again.

They were close enough now to see the Gardeners. One man, one woman, moving at a jog. The man was Glendin, a bald and quiet man, member of the Garden Council; she'd spoken with him briefly before. The distance closed rapidly, and they stopped when they met.

"Murdergirl, Harissa," Glendin said. "Are you hurt? Has the desert kept you?"

The woman, her short, black fringe of hair casting a shadow on her face, held her torch close to Harissa. "Your forehead."

"I'm fine, Iola," Harissa said. "It's getting better."

"What happened?" Iola asked.

"Skinheads," Murdergirl answered. Iola and Glendin looked at each other. "What is it?" Murdergirl asked.

"Hux was attacked by the Skinheads as well. Maybe the same ones."

Harissa shook her head. "Murdergirl killed them both."

"Good," Glendin said. "Two less Skinheads to trouble the Valley." He spat on the ground.

"How is Hux?" Murdergirl asked, and started walking toward the Garden again. They did not answer.

"Iola?" Harissa asked.

"Bad," Glendin responded for Iola.

"They're becoming too bold," Iola said. The six members of the Garden council sat in a circle. Because Murdergirl and Harissa had been attacked by Skinheads and were close to the situation, they were invited to sit in, making eight.

"Bold?" Glendin said. "Bold is taking two drinks of water when your mother says one. They're desperate. Their food must be lacking. You know they eat almost nothing besides their skin horses."

"It's not just that," a quiet voice said. Everyone turned to look at Hux. He sat on the sand, bandages wrapped around his torso and half of his face, covering one eye. His own blood stained his clothes. "They've gone crazy. They were already half there, risking their lives with that poison meat, wearing the skins of the dead on their own bodies. But now…" He stared ahead, unfocused.

Rebecca laid a hand on his shoulder. "You don't have to speak. Rest."

He shook his head. "They came out of nowhere, two of them. And for nothing. The water I was bringing from the River, they even let it pour out onto the sand, wasted. I escaped in the darkness. Otherwise…" He shook his head again, and closed his eyes.

"It was the same with us," Murdergirl said. "They came out of nowhere. Just the two."

"It's a message they're sending," Glendin said.

"A message?" Iola asked. "The Skinheads?"

"Maybe the message isn't from them," Murdergirl said.

"Then who?" Iola asked.

Hambone's grinning white teeth flashed in her mind. "You took me in," she said. "You saved me from death, from the Bones, after what I did to them."

Iola put up her hand. "Murdergirl, please. The Skinheads and Hambone working together? That's as likely as the Worms working with us."

Glendin laughed and nodded his head.

"Once," Murdergirl said, "I was lost in the desert, in the middle of a sandstorm at night. I stumbled on an abandoned Worm coffin and stayed in it 'til the morning, it kept me safe. Hambone could have stumbled on the Skinheads just the same."

Harissa caught her eye, and then looked at their torch bundles, still unopened, hiding the bicycle spears.

"We need to fight," Murdergirl said. "They've attacked me and Harissa on a run for torches, Hux on a run for water. We weren't harming them, only getting supplies for ourselves."

"But you have survived," Rebecca said.

"Barely." Murdergirl pointed at Hux, his eyes still closed. "If we give them this, they will take more."

"What are you saying we should do?" Glendin asked. "Attack the Skinheads?"

"I have my shotgun," Murdergirl said. "Tonight I killed two Skinheads with it. I have enough shells to kill a hundred more. And from the Forge, we can get more weapons. Metal spears, light and sharp, enough for all of us."

"You want to go to the Skinhead farm near the city?" Iola asked. "Even the desert itself is poisoned there, and every step is one closer to death."

"But waiting is also one step closer to death," Glendin said. "If they come again—"

"They will not come again," Rebecca said. "We have been careless, it's true. One person going to the river is vulnerable, and so are two going to the Forge. We will increase the amount going out together; threes, fours, fives. We are Gardeners, we are strong because we are together."

"What if they come here, to the Garden?" Glendin asked.

Rebecca pondered. Murdergirl saw the old woman's eyes look over her right shoulder, where the shotgun waited. "Skinheads in the Garden would be unheard of," Rebecca said. "You may as well ask what we should do if the river runs on the surface of the desert."

"What would we do?" Glendin pressed.

"We have more torches. We will extend the perimeter, double the torches. You know the Skinheads will not come to the flame."

"Before," Murdergirl said, "I was told that they would not attack anyone holding a torch. But they attacked us. Maybe Hux is right, that they've gone crazy, like a rabid hyena."

Rebecca lowered her gray head and spread her hands. "That could be right. If anyone would go crazy, it is a Skinhead. And we all know that the only way to stop a rabid hyena is to kill it. But, you do not go to him. To do so is only to put yourself at risk. You stay where you are strong—here, in the Garden—and if he comes to us, then we can finish him easily, by only one blow from each of us. I can see," she said, looking at Harissa, "that some of you are not convinced. When the Bones come again, I will speak to Hambone."

"What could he do?" Iola asked.

Glendin smiled and shook his head. "We give him food in trade for protection, don't we? Maybe he should actually provide that protection."

Iola nodded slightly. "If the Bones actually protected us, the Skinheads wouldn't be a problem."

Murdergirl looked at each member of the council in the faint light of the breaking sun. They were Gardeners, not fighters. Glendin would fight, with the backing of the rest, but the others were relaxed now that Rebecca had spoken. Iola would follow Glendin. Hux... perhaps Hux would fight alongside her, but the Skinheads had put a stop to that before it had started, and it would be days or weeks before he could walk, nevermind wield a weapon. And without the council, the rest of the Garden would not fight.

Chapter 14

Murdergirl sat in her tent with Harissa. She cleaned the girl's injured forehead again and bandaged it.

"What do you think we should do?" Harissa asked, as Murdergirl wrapped the white bandage around her head.

"It doesn't matter what I think," Murdergirl said. "If the council does not agree, we cannot do it. And on my own—"

"I would help."

"I know you would." Murdergirl smiled. "But even with you, tough as you are, we are still only two."

"Your gun makes us a lot stronger. We could do it. We could go to the Skinhead farm and stop them."

"It's too dangerous. Like Iola said, even the desert there is poison."

"How could the desert be poisoned? 'The desert helps us all', right? And if nobody has been there, how do they know it's poisoned?"

Murdergirl considered. "Well, surely someone has been there. The Garden has existed for a long time. People must have gone out all over the Valley."

Harissa shook her head. "They won't go anywhere. They think everything is here for them."

"'They'?"

"Gardeners."

Murdergirl raised her eyebrows.

"Yes, I know I'm a Gardener, too. But I'm not like all the rest. I don't *want* to be here forever. I want to go places. I want to do things."

"What things? What places?"

"Now you're talking like one of them," Harissa said. "They say there is nothing out there. Just sand, then mountains, then a poisoned world. Well, I know there has to be more. There has to be more, and if there isn't more then there *could* be more. And if we don't do something about the Skinheads, you know they'll be back. They eat people, you know. It's not just a story."

"Have you seen them do it?"

"Imagine if it was Hux. What if he hadn't been so fast, he hadn't got away? What if they chewed the flesh right off his face and we didn't find him until the sun had turned his bones white."

Murdergirl turned her face away, as if she had seen it happen right in front of her.

"We will talk to the council," she said. "Try to convince them."

"I've been trying to convince them my whole life," Harissa replied. "Or since the summer last year, at least. Nothing happens here." Harissa picked at her fingernails. "Sometimes I think even being a Bone would be better."

Murdergirl's head snapped up. "Never think that."

"You were."

It was true. She'd thought the same. Thought that being a Bone was better, at least she wasn't starving, at least she was doing something, being *someone*. "I was wrong. The Bones... listen, they're one step above Skinheads, but it's only a tiny step. The only thing they believe is that someone strong gets to own anyone weaker. They steal from the

Garden, not because they have to, but because they want to. They like it." After every raid on the Garden, or every 'visit', as Hambone called it, the Bones laughed about how easy it was, how the Gardeners never resisted. Rebecca was the only one who ever said anything against Hambone, but never forcefully.

"But at least they're doing *something*," Harissa said. "What do we do here?" She shrugged. "Grow plants. Eat fruit. Keep water a secret."

"Harissa, it's more than that. The Garden creates life. With what you grow here, you keep the whole valley alive."

"Not the Skinheads."

"Right, listen..." Murdergirl pinched the bridge of her nose. "You're not thinking about becoming a Skinhead next, are you?"

"No, of course not."

"Then let's leave them out of it."

"There's nothing to do here, and we do nothing!"

"Trust me, it's no better with the Bones. They have no goals, nothing to work towards. At least here in the Garden, you plan things around a yearly harvest, you work towards that."

"For fifteen years, I've done that. And no, not since I was a toddler, but close enough. Where has it got us? Bones taking more and more food. The Skinheads becoming more dangerous. They almost killed me, and what have I done with my life?"

"You know, when I was your age—a few years before my mother was killed—I lived in the desert. It was all I'd ever known. She kept me away from all the groups. Skinheads, Forge, Garden, Oasis. It was hard—"

"You're not convincing me," Harissa said, accompanied by a roll of her eyes.

"Let me finish. It was hard, but it was never boring. We lived so close to the edge, there was no chance to become bored. Sometimes we might get lucky and have enough food to last a week, more often we might go a week with no food. It felt like we truly had a goal—survival; just having that goal made you feel alive every day."

Harissa was watching her face, listening intently.

"That whole time, what I secretly wanted, without even knowing what it was, was the Garden. Food every day. Safety in numbers. Time to relax. And now that I have it, wow, it's good. When I got here, it was like waking up from a dream and you're still in it. You can't know that, because you've always had this. But..." she held up her hand, seeing Harissa becoming restless, "...I know it will not last. There isn't the same vibrancy to life, where all the colors and smells and tastes become bright and precious because you're fighting for them. You can be born here, live here, grow old and die here, and everything is the same for your whole life. It's safe... usually, but is it living?"

"Some people like it this way," Harissa said. "It isn't so bad."

"Right, but..." Murdergirl stopped, and laughed. "You don't have to start defending it now, I'm not attacking it. The Garden is great. I like it here. Listen, I promised you I'd take you to the bunker. We'll see the lectric lights. I'll take you on the motorcycle. And after that... we'll see."

"What if Rebecca says no?"

"Well, it's not really up to her, is it? You're a Gardener, you're free to go where you want."

"And what about the Skinheads? Do you really think putting up more torches is going to keep us safe? Hux didn't have a torch, but we did, and they still attacked us. What if you hadn't been there? What if..." Harissa's expression crumpled inwards, tears at the corners of her eyes.

Murdergirl put her arm around Harissa. Sobs shook the girl's body. The answer to her question was clear, and Harissa certainly knew it herself, though Murdergirl wasn't about to say it out loud—the Skinheads would have killed her. They would have eaten her, probably while she was still alive, like the hyenas had done to the unfortunate but deserving Skinhead that Murdergirl had wounded. Then they would have sliced and peeled the skin and hair from her skull, and worn it as a mask; her beautiful red hair would have made it quite a prize.

"It's not right," Murdergirl said. "But we'll fix it."

Harissa's crying slowed and her tears dried up. She coughed and sniffled and cleared her throat.

"How?"

Even in the middle of the Garden, they were still on their own in this matter. Until Hux recovered, there was nobody who would join them, and even he wasn't a sure thing.

"I don't know," Murdergirl replied. "But we will."

The Garden always kept its inhabitants busy. The end of the major harvest meant endless drying of fruit. Every piece, laid out in the sun on sheets of cactus fiber, turned regularly to dry evenly on all sides. With the moisture gone, the fruit would last for months.

Small swarms of insects saw it as their job to relieve the Gardeners of their excess fruit. Murdergirl was one of those assigned to keep them away. Like most work in the Garden, it was repetitive. Marching back and forth along a line of fruit, waving palm leaves at the insects that approached. Twenty steps one way, turn, twenty steps the other way. Some insects managed to settle on the fruit, but an extra wave sent them on their way. Occasionally, a particularly intelligent insect realized that Murdergirl was the source of the waving leaf, and gave her an indignant bite; this being its last act before she squashed it with a swift, open palm.

Every creature fought for survival against others. The Bones' idea that those who were bigger and stronger always won was right. The little insects stood no chance against her, not on their own. They could bite her, and it hurt a little, but it was no threat. But if they could all work together, if the five thousand insects in the air around the Garden all came with the same purpose, they could drive her and the other Gardeners from the fruit and take it. But they never would.

Twenty steps, turn, twenty steps, digging a trench in the sand with the motion of her feet. At a turn, she made eye contact with Harissa, working several rows away. How would it feel after a decade of this?

Towards noon, she stopped for an early lunch and went to visit Hux in his tent. She met Rebecca coming out.

"How is he?"

"Healing," Rebecca said. "Fast, like you, when the desert brought you to us." She smiled, the corners of her eyes a hundred wrinkles. When her smile left, most of the wrinkles stayed. "I know you don't approve of the way we do things."

"I don't… there isn't…"

"It's okay. This isn't the Bones. You don't have to agree with me." She closed her eyes and bowed her head slightly. "I know I am not perfect, there's no need for either of us to pretend I am. Maybe this decision we made is the wrong one. But it is our decision. The Gardeners are peaceful. We work, we love, we eat. We help others, as the desert helps us all."

They work, they love, they eat. Nothing more, nothing less. But she wanted more. And she wanted nothing more. The hint of tears stung her eyes.

The old woman reached her rough, wrinkled hand up to Murdergirl's face. She gently stroked her cheek. "You are not a Gardener," she said. "There is something in you that will never be content. I know it. I see it. I have seen it in Harissa for years. I thought, enough time given, she would settle. And, enough time given, maybe she would. Thirty years, forty years. When she goes with you, I hope you both find what you are seeking. Only try to keep her safe."

"I'm not taking her anywhere." Except the bunker. "Well, not for long. And she wouldn't leave the Garden, she wouldn't leave you." Would she? "You're a grandmother to her, almost a mother."

Rebecca smiled. "No, perhaps she wouldn't. But," she looked up at the sun, eyes squinted, "how many more days will I be here? Sometimes, on a chilly morning, I feel it in my bones. I feel the end coming. And I don't want Harissa to live for my memory. And you," she said, pointing at Murdergirl, "you also must get what you're after. Be the person you are. Not a Bone, not a Gardener. Not a Skinhead, not a Forgemate. Be who you are."

"Rebecca, I don't know..." Murdergirl sighed. She felt a familiar ache in her chest and in her throat. Faded some since its peak years ago, but never gone forever. Who was she?

"You're Murdergirl," Rebecca said. "Just like you told me when we first met."

"I don't even know what that means. It's just something the Bones thought up, likely when they were drunk. Murdergirl, Murderboy. Hambone probably thought it was a good joke."

"Well, the clue is in the name itself." Rebecca patted Murdergirl's back, where her shotgun would rest.

Murdergirl raised an eyebrow, but Rebecca continued talking before she could ask what the old woman meant.

"And speaking of Hambone," Rebecca said, "what do you think he will say if I ask for protection?"

Murdergirl shrugged. "You know he doesn't really want to protect the Garden, right? He only says that to make it seem more like… like he's in charge, like his job is to be the one in control. Maybe it makes him feel better about what he does."

"I know that."

"But maybe. The Bones are always looking for something to do. Part of the reason they come to the Garden sometimes, it's just for something to do. Going to the Skinhead farm, that would be something to do. But it would also be dangerous, and they're not going to put themselves at risk."

"I will ask, either way," Rebecca said. "What's the worst that can happen? Now go on, see Hux. He could use a visit from you."

Murdergirl ducked inside the tent flap. Hux lay in bed, face still bandaged and his one visible eye closed, his rough, slender-fingered hands at his sides. When she'd first heard

Hux had been attacked by the Skinheads, she'd immediately feared they had killed him. It must have been a close thing. Just like with Harissa, they'd hit him in the face. But Gardeners never took a torch when they went to the river, and the darkness had saved him, had helped him escape. If he was well, would he go to the bunker with them? Would he think it was a strange question if she asked? Picturing the three of them walking together in the desert scratched an itch that she had almost forgotten.

His breathing was peaceful. Had there been two Skinheads? If it had been three, he might not have escaped. Like Harissa said, they'd have eaten the flesh right off his bones. She reached out to stroke the uninjured side of his face. A lifetime in the desert, and still his skin looked smooth. He opened his eye, and she put her hand on his shoulder instead.

"I can see out of my other eye, you know," he said. "I've been watching you, while you watch me."

"I haven't been watching you," she said.

One corner of his mouth pulled up. "Maybe it's just me, then. I could see the shape of you through the bandage. The way your hair lays over your shoulder and spills down your chest. The white glow of the sun around you."

His one eye seemed to see right through her. She looked away and cleared her throat. "Rebecca says you're healing." So hard to say anything real to him. Perhaps he could hear it even if she didn't say it.

He nodded slightly, tucking his chin into his chest. "My head doesn't feel so bad. Only a little headache sometimes. I see the way people look at me, so I assume it looks worse than it feels. But where they shot me…" he shifted his body and winced. "Still feels like flame right through me."

"They shot you? The Skinheads?"

He nodded again and spread his hands. "Where did the Skinheads get a gun, I know the question already. Probably just a zip-pistol, not an old gun, though I was a bit busy and didn't have time to check."

"They've never used guns before," she said. "I guess it does fit with everything else the Skinheads do, using a zip-pistol that's almost as likely to kill you as whoever you're shooting. But would they make one themselves?"

"They meet other people, I suppose. I don't know who would want to meet a Skinhead, but someone must. Someone in the Bones, maybe. I know everything is supposed to be dead beyond the mountains, but I think there must be people there, mountain men." He shrugged. "If they go into the mountains—and wouldn't the Skinheads, even though it's dangerous, even though it's deadly?—they can meet with others and get zip-pistols."

"Skinheads with guns," Murdergirl said. "I can't think of anything worse for the valley. If it's true, who is to stop them? The council won't fight, the people of the Oasis won't fight. The Forge-mates would fight, but only if you could get the enemy actually to their rock fortress; they're not going to leave it. There's only me. And Harissa."

"And me," Hux said. He moved to sit up, but stopped halfway with a grimace and eased himself back down.

"I hoped you would be on our side."

"Anybody who is on the side of the Valley, anybody who doesn't want to see every grain of sand soaked in blood, they should be on your side. The Garden wants peace, but we can't have it if the Skinheads and the Bones want violence. They can't see it. I couldn't see it myself until it happened to me. But there is something possible beyond this."

Murdergirl put her hand on his. "Would you go with us? Me and Harissa?"

"When I'm better. Rebecca says a few more days. A week, maybe. Where would we go?"

"Not far. Not at first." A smile rose on her face. Was this what she had been searching for? On her own, she was not enough. And a group as big as the Garden, maybe too much. But three—or maybe four, one day. She looked away from him. He linked his fingers with hers.

Shouting grabbed their attention. Murdergirl listened and furrowed her brow.

"Those don't sound like Gardeners," Hux said.

"Bones." Murdergirl moved to go, but Hux kept his grip on her hand.

"Stay," he said. "Remember, they don't know you're here. They'll get food, and they'll go."

A scream from outside. Harissa. She pulled her hand away from Hux, and he released her, but his uncovered eye pleaded with her. She opened the tent flap and stepped out.

Rebecca stood at the Garden pool. Hambone was near her, standing several heads taller than the old woman with the bent back, and his hat standing taller still. Murdergirl could see a large group of Bones, twenty or thirty, scattered around the Garden. Maybe others that she couldn't see. They usually only came with ten or so.

"You're supposed to be protecting us," Rebecca said. "Where is that protection? You leave that girl alone."

"Now, now, there's no need for all this commotion," Hambone said. He waved his hand to the Bone who held

Harissa; the man released his grip. Her shirt was torn off one shoulder.

"We're here, aren't we?" Hambone said, and grinned. "Ain't nothing bad gonna happen with all of us keeping you so safe like this. But you've had a nice peaceful time. Been months, hasn't it? I hear the Garden has had a good harvest, and we're only here to get what's ours."

Rebecca pointed her finger at him. "The Skinheads have been attacking us. They almost killed Hux. And Harissa." She jabbed him in the chest.

Hambone took half a step back. "Rebecca, you know I don't control what those half-men do."

"What about your own? What about you? Are you any more than half a man yourself?"

Hambone removed his hat. He looked at Rebecca a moment, and his grin got wider, all white teeth but nothing behind it. "As long as we've started out this way, I'd say you aren't putting up your end of the bargain either." He shook his finger at her. "Ain't that right?"

"We have your food—"

He waggled his head. "We'll get to the food. That, plus extra. Now..." He bowed his legs out to get closer to eye level with Rebecca, "...what about water? I hear there's a whole pile of water you've got, and you've been holding out on old Hambone."

Rebecca looked at the Garden pool. "This water is for the trees. There is only enough for it, and for us."

"Mmm, mmm, mmm, that's not what I heard." He closed his eyes and swayed, hearing his own music. Then his eyes opened. "I heard it's a river." He moved his hand across between them, palm open. "Wide as ten men. Enough to drown every person here. That's right, drowning. You heard of it?" He raised his eyebrows, still grinning. "People used to drown all the time, so I hear." He tilted his head forward. "You know what drowning is, Rebecca?"

The old woman frowned at him.

"World used to have so much water it could kill you!" Hambone shouted. "And now, look at us." He threw his hands up. "Everybody with their faces turned up on the few days it rains, saying oh, ain't we so lucky. How many years we been doing this, Rebecca? I remember when your back used to be straight. You could stand up tall, look me in the eye. And now?" He looked down at her and shrugged. "And that whole time, there's been this river."

Rebecca slowly shook her head. "Look around you, Hambone. You crazy fool. Do you see anything but this little pool, this little stream, just a drop of water in the desert?"

"Ah." He raised his finger up. "Of course, I'm not stupid, you're not stupid, none of us is stupid. This river, it's under the desert. Maybe it's always been there, since the before times, maybe before the before times. Maybe they didn't even know. But you found it." He reached out his open hand and then snapped it shut into a fist. "And you kept it. Meanwhile, everybody else is thirsty." He licked his lips. "George, you thirsty?" he called over his shoulder.

"Powerful thirsty, boss," the man who had grabbed Harissa said.

"Murderboy, you thirsty?"

"You know I am, Hambone," Murderboy called back, stepping out from between two tents. Murdergirl felt her fist tighten on its own. He'd had the chance to leave the Bones. The chance to help. On that day when she'd confronted Hambone, Murderboy could have made all the difference. How many times had she tried to get through to him, tried to talk about why things were the way they were, and if they could change? But he never said anything different, never wavered. Maybe he couldn't.

"Now," Hambone said, "do we have any volunteers? Anybody who wants to experience first-hand what drowning is?" He spread his arms out, palms up, and spun around slowly. "Might be the first person in a hundred years to drown, it's quite an opportunity. Hmm. Nobody?" He looked back at Rebecca. "Everybody says how eager the Gardeners always are to help out, but now when little old Hambone needs a hand, I can't hear anything but pocket mice." His smile dropped away. "George," he said, pointing to Harissa, "bring me that one."

George grabbed Harissa's arm and pulled her.

"Let me go!" she shouted. She struggled against him, but he was bigger, stronger. She swung with her free hand and punched him in the face. It staggered him, and she shook free. She ran two steps, straight into Murderboy. He locked his arm around her neck and squeezed. George grabbed her arm again, and together they brought her towards Hambone.

Murdergirl cursed silently. Murderboy and George forced Harissa to her knees at the Garden pool.

"Hambone, what is this?" Rebecca asked. "This isn't our deal. Just take your food and go."

"Old woman, you know what the deal really is. Look around you. How many of us are there, strong, and how many of you are there, weak? All of us are strong. All of you are weak. And the weak have been hiding things from the strong, haven't they? I figure maybe we've been too easy on you; you begin to think that Hambone is weak, too."

Murdergirl had her shotgun. Hadn't taken it off since that night in the desert with the Skinheads. Loaded with two shells, and plenty more spare. What to do? She knew the Bones didn't really want a fight, and if the Gardeners fought back, the Bones would leave. But they might have missed their chance. There were too many of the Bones. Too close together. The Gardeners had let them all right in, thinking they could trade food for their lives like usual, even though there were so many more Bones than usual. She looked around. Who would fight? She spotted Glendin. Maybe him. She tried to catch his eye, but he was watching Hambone.

Hambone put his boot between Harissa's shoulder blades and shoved her. She fell forward, her face splashed in the pool. Murderboy put his knee on the small of her back, George held her wrists. She wriggled and kicked, but it was hopeless for her. She held her head up, just a few inches above the water. Murderboy placed his hand against the back of her head and pressed her face down into the water. She bucked against them, jerked her head back above water, and with the last air in her lungs screamed, "Murdergirl!" before Murderboy forced her head under again.

No time to plan. No more time left at all. She stepped forward, and slung the shotgun off her back.

Chapter 15

"Let her go, Hambone," Murdergirl said.

Hambone swung his head toward her. For just a split-second, his jaw hung slack, and then his face formed into a grin again.

"Well now, if it isn't my prodigal daughter, back from the dead. I figured you'd been eaten by worms and turned into sand yourself, rejoining the desert from whence ye came, and so on. But look at you." He cocked his head. "Right as rain. Come to rejoin the fold?"

Harissa fought against the two men holding her down, splashing her arms wildly in the pool. Her screams bubbled up from the water.

Murdergirl aimed the shotgun at Hambone's head.

Hambone shook his finger at her. "No time to chat?" He tilted his head towards Harissa. "Because of this little girl?" He stroked his chin. "Alright, you've persuaded me. Mmm." He bent down and tapped George and Murderboy each on the shoulder, then jerked his head back, indicating for them to move. Harissa pushed herself shakily to one knee. She coughed and gulped in air. Her red hair lay in a dripping mess across her face and clung to her neck. She looked back and forth between Hambone and Murdergirl.

"You see?" Hambone said to Murdergirl. "Nothing that a little civility can't fix."

Murdergirl took her hand off the barrel of the shotgun, and motioned for Harissa to come to her. Harissa rose to her feet and took one faltering step. Hambone whipped his gun out of his waistband and pointed it at Rebecca's head.

"Go, girl," Rebecca said, her voice steady. Harissa splashed through the pond to reach Murdergirl's side.

"Ain't this just a tasty situation?" Hambone asked. "Who's getting shot this time, do you think?"

"Are you okay?" Murdergirl whispered to Harissa. The girl nodded; no tears in her eyes, only anger.

"It's not too late, Hambone," Murdergirl said. "Take the Bones, leave. Take your food, even. Nobody has to die."

Hambone sighed loudly, tilting his face to the sky. "Murdergirl, Murdergirl. Look at you. Pointing a gun at me, telling me nobody has to die. Why point a gun if you don't want to shoot? Last time you did that, I believe dear old Davey died."

"Davey died because he was an idiot, and he shot first. Are you an idiot?"

"Direct, as usual. Maybe I am an idiot. I let you in the Bones, maybe because you have your mother's eyes." A little smile from him. "And then I did let you go, after all, when I could have killed you, way back when you wanted to stop Davey sowing his seed in someone's back garden even when they'd already agreed, tried to upset the whole natural order of things. But that's all in the past, I don't hold it against you. Someone always has to die. When a hyena goes out for lunch, that means the end is here for someone else. We all die. You can't keep people alive, not even the ones you love, like little red-head over there. For a time, sure. But the desert always gets what it wants."

"You're just talking nonsense, Hambone. Maybe it sounds like something to the Bones. Maybe it sounded like something to me, once. But now I know it, and I'm sure you know it—it's nonsense. A breeze blowing through, leaving nothing, taking nothing."

Hambone pressed the barrel of his gun against Rebecca's temple, the pressure bending her neck to the side.

Rebecca nodded at Murdergirl. *Go,* she mouthed silently.

Go? She couldn't leave Rebecca, couldn't leave the other Gardeners. Hux, still laid in his tent. But there were too many Bones. She had plenty of shells, had always kept a bag tied at her waist since the night the Skinheads attacked. She could kill a few of them. Five. Ten, if she was lucky and they were slow. But it would end the same.

"I believe I see the problem, now," Hambone said. With his gun still pressed against the side of Rebecca's head, he slowly swept his other hand around, indicating the whole of the Garden. "All of you know where this river is. And yet, none of you will say."

"That's right," Rebecca said. "Nobody is ever going to tell you."

"Oh, so now there is a river? Here I am, being generous, giving you all the chance to simply get this over with, and you're telling me, to my face." He winked at Rebecca. "Audacious. Simply audacious! And that's the problem. You think, simply because I have been kind up to this point, because I have been gentle—aren't I a gentle soul, George?"

"Yes, boss."

"Because I have been gentle, because I haven't simply slaughtered each and every one of you where you stand, you think I can't. You think I won't. You think you've seen inside me and that I'm like you, way on deep down. Well." He looked directly at Murdergirl. His smile slipped away. "I ain't."

Hambone pulled the trigger.

Chapter 16

Harissa screamed through her tangled, wet hair, reaching out towards Rebecca, but she was already dead, blood pouring down the side of her face. Hambone held the old woman's body in front of him, arm wrapped around her neck, holding her up as if there was some life in her still. Her arms hung slack. The explosion of the gunshot had quieted everything around, even the pocket mice. Harissa stepped towards Hambone. Several Bones pulled out zip-pistols.

Murdergirl jerked Harissa back. The girl struggled, trying to wriggle free of Murdergirl's grasp. "It's too late," Murdergirl said. "We have to go."

"We can't leave her," Harissa said.

"We'll come back," Murdergirl said. Would they? Could they?

Harissa came, crying quietly. Murdergirl walked backwards, slowly, shotgun still aimed at Hambone. Her finger shook on the trigger. Her whole body shook; every part of her wanted to kill that fucking bastard. They would kill her then, but so what? It almost felt worth it. But Rebecca had wanted her to go, to take Harissa, to save the girl that was like her own flesh and blood. And for that, she had to leave everything.

They were past Hux's tent. He had surely heard everything. She wanted to go in to him, to call out to him, but it would only draw the attention of the Bones. If he was lucky, the Bones wouldn't find him, wouldn't hurt him, he was no threat to them lying in bed.

"Where you gonna go, girl?" Hambone called out, still holding Rebecca's corpse as a shield. He said something to George and Murderboy. They each went separately, George to the right and Murderboy to the left, out of sight.

Murdergirl and Harissa were in the tangle of tents where the Gardeners lived, with narrow passageways between them.

Even out of sight, Hambone's voice still came. "There's only the desert for you out there."

Which way to the motorcycle? It was a maze among the tents, and they had to be careful.

"You're still a Bone, Murdergirl. Give us the girl, and nobody will lay a hand on you. You have my word."

His word. Murdergirl almost laughed out loud. Ahead, at a turn in the tent passages, a Bone stood with his back to them. She put her hand on Harissa to stop the girl, and put her finger to her own lips. As quietly as she could, she padded towards the Bone. She'd seen him before. He had a hairstyle you couldn't forget, shaved close except for a strip right down the middle. She probably had spoken to him even, when she was with the Bones.

Had to be quiet, couldn't shoot him, couldn't let him shout and alert the others. She felt the sand crunching under her feet with each slow step, but he didn't turn. She couldn't remember his name. Couldn't picture his face. It was better that way. She swapped the shotgun around in her hands, so she was holding it by the barrel. With only a few steps to go, she rushed forward and raised the gun up.

The Bone turned at the sudden noise and stepped back. His face showed fear. Recognition. The start of a smile, almost. She brought the gun down on his forehead, a grunt escaping her from the effort. He dropped, blood leaking from his nose and ears. His face still held that little smile. Chuck, that was his name. Chuckles is what they'd called him. She went back to Harissa and pulled the girl along.

"It ends the same for everyone out there," Hambone's voice came again. "If a hyena doesn't get you, it's a cripple snake. Sometimes a cripple snake first, then a hyena finds you while you're still alive but can't move."

She could picture Hambone's grinning face. If only it was *his* head she'd smashed with the gun, bashed his teeth in, unloaded both barrels into his body.

Every tent looked the same, white fabric flapping above a patch of sand. She peered around a corner. Clear, but which way? Harissa knew the layout of the Garden better. She tapped the girl on the shoulder, pointed each way, raised her eyebrows questioningly. No response. Harissa's eyes were red. Tears streamed down her wet face.

"The Garden belongs to us now," Hambone shouted. "Nobody goes out without me saying so." The barrel of the shotgun was cold and heavy in her hand. If it came to that, it would be her gun doing the asking.

She went left, pulling Harissa with her. Just a few steps away, from around the next tent came a Bone, one she didn't recognize, a new recruit or just one not worth remembering. A rusted zip-pistol stuck out from his waistband at the front. Her jaw tightened. Only one way out—through him.

"Let's not do anything crazy," he said. His hand shifted towards the zip-pistol. Too late.

Murdergirl pulled the trigger. The shell exploded out, filling his body and head with shot. No hiding where they were now, every Bone in the Garden would have heard that gunshot. They stepped forward over the Bone's bloody corpse. She wished it was Hambone lying there staining the desert red. One day it would be. One fucking day, Hambone.

Around another corner. Four more white tents, sand paths leading between them. How many tents were there in this place? They had to be close, but she was never going to find the right way on her own. She stopped.

"Harissa, I need you with me." Harissa looked at her, unfocused. "Which way to the motorcycle?" Harissa looked away. "Harissa, please. I know it's awful. Rebecca is gone. I know that. But you know she died to save you. She wanted you out of here, she wanted you safe."

Tears streamed down Harissa's face. She brought her hand up, pointing ahead of them. They went straight on. This time when Murdergirl poked her head around a corner, she saw an open space. Bamboo crates piled all around. A few Bones, too.

She crouched down, pulling Harissa with her. She motioned forward, pointing to the stack of crates where the motorcycle hid and waited. Harissa nodded. Then they were out, keeping low. To the side, a Bone she hadn't seen. George. They both went down, flat, behind a few crates.

The Bones spoke to each other while they looked.

"Anything?" the one near them asked.

"No, you idiot." Murderboy's voice. "You think I'd just be standing here, a couple lady Gardeners caught, and not say anything?"

"Well, whatever. I was just asking."

"Ask me when you've got something worth asking."

She heard the one nearby move away. Staying low to the ground, they crawled towards the motorcycle, slipped between the crates. Out of sight for the moment.

"Did you see that little red-haired one?" George asked. "As white and fresh as one of these tents. Whew. Makes me sweat just thinking about what I'd do with her."

"You always sweat, that's why there's not a single woman in this desert wants to touch you."

Murdergirl slid the canvas off the motorcycle as carefully as they could; it still made a rumpling noise.

"You hear that?"

"I hear the sound of that little one vomiting, thinking about your sweaty balls even coming near her."

"You got a problem with me?"

"Everyone has a problem with you. They just don't say anything 'cause they're know you're going to cry about it."

A pause.

"Listen," George said, "you can't—oh, fuck it." The dull thud of one person's fist colliding with the flesh of another person.

Murdergirl swung her leg over the motorcycle. Patted the seat behind her and Harissa climbed on. Murdergirl gave her ponytail a tug and turned the metal.

The beast woke up with a rumbling roar. It exploded into her body from below, spreading to her fingertips. Kickstand up. Turn the handle, give it power. The motorcycle lurched forward, knocking bamboo crates aside. The two Bones stood looking, mouths gaping, Murderboy with a spot of blood at his lip. Murdergirl steered right for them and they dove to the side.

Harissa held on tight, Murdergirl gave the beast more power and sped out of the Garden. Every Bone, every

Gardener turned to see. The *crack, crack* of zip-pistols reached her ears. Nobody was going to hit them moving that fast, especially not with those hand-made guns. Hambone stood at the Garden pool over Rebecca's body. He held his pistol at his side, did not aim at them. Because he knew it was pointless? So many chances he'd had to kill her, every one of them missed.

Glendin grabbed the Bone nearest to him around the neck, punching him in the face with his other fist while the Bone struggled. The other Bones didn't notice, too focused on the spectacle of Murdergirl and Harissa on the motorcycle. Another Gardener attacked a Bone with a zip-pistol, wrestled it away. Not even a zip-pistol could miss from right against your head. The Bone's brains spread out behind him. Another Bone saw, shot the Gardener as well. Bone and Gardener lay tangled together, a bloody waste.

Murdergirl made a wide circle of the Garden, keeping a safe distance. Two Bones going in Hux's tent. She almost turned towards them, but stopped herself. Steered away instead. She had to get Harissa away, had to get her safe. If they killed Hux… she pushed that thought out of her head. Turned away from the Garden, into the open desert.

Chapter 17

Sand raced away beneath the wheels of the beast. The Garden lay far behind them, out of sight. Out here it felt like there was nothing else. No sound but the steady roar of the motorcycle, a rumble that they held between their thighs. Far off in the distance, mountains ringed the valley. The sun shone full on them, with no clouds in the sky, but they rode fast, and the wind kept them cool. Murdergirl wanted to keep going forever, to never stop. Just them and the motorcycle, the desert and the sky.

Harissa's body shivered against her. Murdergirl's first time with a passenger. This wasn't how it was supposed to be. They were supposed to be going out, just for a little while, just for a ride, maybe a visit to the bunker, and then back to the Garden. Harissa should be laughing, whooping, loving the thrill of riding the beast. Harissa still held on to her, but less tightly now, head laid against her back. At the start she'd felt the wetness of tears, but that had dried up, either from the wind or because Harissa's tears had stopped. You couldn't cry forever. The wind and the roar of the motorcycle made talking impossible. You'd have to shout, and what had happened wasn't something to shout about. That was a blessing; she didn't want to talk. Once again, she'd let Hambone live, even after he killed Rebecca. And he'd killed her right in front of Harissa. What was she thinking? What must that feel like? Well, she knew. Same thing had happened to her, when her mother was killed. She hadn't seen it, but she'd heard. And just like Rebecca and

Harissa, her mother had only wanted her to be away, to be safe.

After the Skinheads attacked, she'd told herself she wouldn't be without shells for her shotgun, and she hadn't been. The bag of shells still sat on her hip. Enough to kill every Bone that had come to the Garden. But what difference had it made? All that power she held, and she hadn't used it.

How long had they been riding? Without the daily routines of the Garden, she had lost track of time.

The cross-top of the Tomb Tree came over the horizon. She hadn't meant to come this way. Hadn't really thought about where they were going, but this was where the beast had led them. When she had been with the Bones, it had taken such a long time to reach the Tree once you saw it. Time to think about how the people before had gathered all their dead into one place, marked them with stones and sticks, most with the cross symbol of death on them.

She turned the metal back and let the motorcycle coast to a stop. The last few turns of the wheels crunched on the sand, and then the desert was completely silent.

Harissa raised her head. "What's going on? Did it die?"

Keep her safe, Rebecca had said.

Murdergirl raised her hand and pointed to the Tomb Tree. "This is the way to the Bones' camp." She let the statement linger, not saying what it meant. It was just a statement of fact—that was the way. But it meant more. They could go there. They could kill the Bones, while the others were in the Garden. They could kill every one of them, tear the camp down, scatter their supplies, let Hambone come back and discover what it felt like to have something taken from you. But it was a crazy idea. It was still just the two of them, a woman and a girl.

"We could..." Harissa paused. "We could go look at it."

Murdergirl looked back over her shoulder at Harissa. "Do you want to?"

Harissa nodded. Murdergirl gave power to the beast, squeezed it between her thighs again. They rumbled towards the Bones' camp. Soon, she could see it, hard edges jutting up from the desert, bamboo and wood from Oasis trees making the frame, burlap hanging down.

She made a wide, lazy circle around it. It didn't look like a place you'd want to live. The Garden and the Oasis had their tents and huts, the Forge-mates had their rock caves, but the Bones had almost nothing, just a few strips of burlap to keep out the worst of the wind and sand. All of their garbage tossed outside in a pile, what they hadn't burned. And she'd been inside, it wasn't any better. The Bones took so much, and what did they do with it? They made things worse for others, didn't even make it good for themselves.

She circled again, closer. The rumble of the motorcycle wasn't something you could miss, not through the barely there walls of the Bones' camp. But nobody came out. Had every Bone gone to the Garden? It couldn't be. There were more. Twenty more, at least. Asleep? The beast would have woken anybody. An ambush, then? There were small holes in the burlap walls, torn due to carelessness, never patched due to laziness. They could be inside; watching, waiting. But they couldn't know she would come here—she hadn't even known herself until she'd seen the Tomb Tree. She gave the motorcycle more power, making the circle tighter around, spraying up sand when she turned, making the beast roar. Still nothing.

The motorcycle came to a stop near the entrance to the camp. Nothing moved inside. Silence in the desert. If there were Bones in there, it couldn't be very many.

"Let's go inside," Harissa said.

"Hang on," Murdergirl said. "We're just having a look, remember?"

"So let's look—inside." Harissa didn't explain her statement either. She didn't have to; Murdergirl knew what it meant. Let's look inside. Let's see who's in there. Let's kill them.

Keep her safe.

Even at the Garden, Harissa hadn't been truly safe. The Bones had just come right in—the Gardeners had let them in, and when they wanted them out it was already too late. There was only one way to keep her safe. Only one way to keep everyone in the Valley safe. Murdergirl slung the shotgun off her back.

Chapter 18

Murdergirl nosed the shotgun into the hanging burlap doorway and pushed it aside. She stepped through, and Harissa followed. She'd tried to leave the girl outside, but Harissa didn't want to miss whatever might happen. And Murdergirl figured she was probably safer staying close, anyway.

The large communal living area at the front was mostly empty. A dozen bamboo crates scattered around for seating, taken from the Garden when the Bones took food. Jugs of wine from the Oasis. A burn barrel stood in the middle, hot ash and glowing coals of wood piled at the bottom. Slabs of slate with hearts and diamonds and flowers scratched on were scattered over a low table, an old game the Bones still played. Murdergirl had never bothered with it, and she'd seen too many fights started over those slates to ever start.

Through another doorway, thin strips of burlap hanging down so you could easily walk through without having to push it. The sleeping area, the sand carpeted with whatever they could find. Some blankets from the before time, mostly full of holes. Sleeping sacks stuffed with bamboo, cactus, and palm fibers. A few animal furs. Those hadn't been here when she was part of the Bones. Animals were poison, everybody knew that. Were their skins and furs poison, too? They must be, the same as a person—you couldn't touch a person with a sickness inside, even if you couldn't see it.

Deeper into the camp, there were a few areas sectioned off. Some for privacy, when they had women. One for

Hambone, who wanted to be alone to think. Hambone's was empty. A sleeping sack. A small crate made of wood from the Oasis—much harder to work with than bamboo—and a book on top with a golden death cross on its black cover. Surely Hambone couldn't read. She picked up the book and flipped through it. Thin pages. No pictures.

They went into another of the private areas. A Bone stood against the wall, holding a shard of rusted metal ready as a weapon. Murdergirl quickly glanced in the corners—nobody else.

"Get out of here," the Bone said. His hands shook. "Hambone is going to be back, he's on his way back." He paused and swallowed. "I think I hear him now."

Murdergirl said nothing, only kept the shotgun pointed at him. He was scared. So he should be.

"Hambone's not going to be happy if he finds you here," he said. "Not after what you did before. He's ready now, he's taking over it all, he's done with the Garden." His face was white.

"Maybe we shouldn't," Harissa said quietly.

"You don't, um... you don't have to do this," the Bone said to Murdergirl..

"Do what?" Harissa asked, shouldering past her. "Did your Bones think about what they didn't have to do when Hambone killed Rebecca?"

"Rebecca..." the Bone licked his dry lips. "So it's already done. But you're not supposed to be here." His eyes brightened and he looked at Murdergirl. "Did Hambone send you?"

Murdergirl shook her head and stepped closer to the Bone. "It's over," she said. "The Bones are finished. There's going to be nothing for Hambone when he gets back here."

“I’ll tell Hambone,” he said. “I’ll pass on your message.” He backed up, pressing against the burlap wall.

Murdergirl pictured Rebecca’s lifeless body. Blood pouring down the old woman’s face from the bullet hole in her head. Hambone’s grinning face, white teeth and a black heart.

“This is the message,” she said. She slowly drew in a breath and pulled the trigger. The Bone slid down the wall, dead, leaving a stain of blood on the burlap.

They rode away slowly, a pillar of smoke rising into the sky from what they had left of the camp.

Chapter 19

Murdergirl sat on the bed. The bunker was different from when she had been here before. It had been comfortable, yes. And safe. But now, with Harissa, it was alive. It was almost... fun. The girl walked around the bunker. She touched things, picked things up.

"You probably shouldn't touch *everything*," Murdergirl said.

"Why not?"

"I don't know. It might break. It's old."

"You're old, but you're not broken."

Murdergirl sighed and smiled. "I'm not old."

"Hux said you lived half again as long as me, and I've been at the Garden forever. So you're half again as old as forever." Before Murdergirl could respond, Harissa said, "It's so bright in here!" She stared up at the lights.

"So, you finally noticed the lectricity? I told you."

Harissa squinted. "It's like having little suns right in the room." She looked away and rubbed her eyes. "Was it like this everywhere before?"

Was it? Did every place have their own lectric lights? The skeletons of the massive buildings in the distance—was there enough lectricity to light them all, plus more? Warm in the winter, cool in the summer. Cold, clean water to drink, always enough food to eat. Plenty of light, even at night; nowhere for a hyena or a desert cat or a cripple snake to hide. No Skinheads.

Every family would've had their own house, just like this. Clean, warm, safe. No rain got in, and no sand, not even a crevice cricket could squeeze under the door. They could have it again, she knew they could. All they had to do was reach out and take it—but everyone had to reach their arm out together. The Bones, the Skinheads, even the Forge's beliefs about tools, they kept everyone at the level they were at now. Living in tents. Afraid of animals. Killing each other for food and water.

A sound. Sandy footsteps above the bunker. Murdergirl was on her feet.

"What is it?" Harissa asked.

Murdergirl stood. A smooth sliding over the sand. Slithering. Snakes. Worms. And then it was gone. She held her breath, closed her eyes.

"Murdergirl?"

She opened her eyes again. Took a breath. "It's nothing," she said. She shook her head and smiled. "Sorry."

Harissa continued poking around, opening boxes, unlocking cases. She could see it in the girl's eyes, and something about her posture, her shoulders; they were free in the bunker, free of worry and fear, at least temporarily. Would she have to bring every person in the desert to the bunker so they could see the lectricity for themselves, so they could experience what humanity had lost and what they could have again?

She looked at Harissa, crouched under the table. "I see now why Pig thought 'pocket mouse' was a good name for you."

Harissa looked back over her shoulder.

"Into everything," Murdergirl said. "Looking for something, but you don't know what."

Harissa held up both hands, full of things she had found.

"Don't let me stop you," Murdergirl said. "Keep going. Maybe there's something useful in those boxes."

Harissa picked up a metal box, which hissed when she opened it. It held dozens of some kind of tubes, each wrapped in green paper. She tore the paper from one of them, and tore the foil underneath that. Each tube held fifteen or twenty little white rings. Harissa put one in her mouth, even as Murdergirl said "Don't!" and sprang off the bed.

Harissa's eyes went wide. "It's hot," she said. "It's cold. No, it's sweet." She smiled. "It's good." She held the tube out to Murdergirl. "Want one?"

Murdergirl looked at the tube. *L-i-f-e-s-a-v-e-r-s.* How long had those been here? A hundred years? More? Even carefully dried fruit wouldn't last more than a few months. Harissa closed her eyes, clearly loving it. Murdergirl took one from the tube and put it in her mouth. Her own eyes went wide. Harissa was right—it was hot, it was cold, it was sweet. It wasn't soft like a fruit, it was hard, almost like a rock. She closed her eyes.

"I told you," Harissa said.

"Just give me another one."

Chapter 20

"Are you sure you want to do this?" Murdergirl asked, her voice raised over the sound of the idling motorcycle. They'd already agreed, talked it over late into the night, but Rebecca's plea for Harissa still echoed in Murdergirl's mind.

"Everyone needs something like the bunker," Harissa replied, tightening her arms around Murdergirl's waist. "A safe place."

Murdergirl tugged her ponytail and gave the beast power. The mountains that ringed the valley loomed ahead, closer than she'd ever seen them. This close up, they blocked out the view of the massive buildings from the humans before. Here, there was only desert and mountain. When they were close enough to the mountains—but not too close—she turned to ride alongside them. What did the Skinhead camp look like? They would probably know it when they saw it.

Along the mountains, areas that could work as paths caught her eye. Some were flat and hard, mostly clear of trees; they had to be from the time before. They were clear enough that it would be possible to take the motorcycle up there, to go over the mountains, past the mountains, to leave the valley. What lay beyond the desert? Anybody who had gone had never returned. Because it was so good that you couldn't bear to come back? She smiled to herself. Not likely. Because the sickness in the ground killed them, or whatever monsters lived there had torn them apart, or a bit of both. If any people did live beyond the mountains, they had to be even crazier than the Skinheads.

Bones littered the desert here. Whole skeletons. Most bleached white by the sun, others still fresh, bits of meat clinging to them. Some were horse, hyena, badger, others she didn't recognize. Most were human. Hundreds of human skeletons, spread all around, more humans than she had ever seen in her life. How many humans were there that lived on the earth, how many hundreds? How big was it, how far past the mountains did it go? What was at the edge? What was *past* the edge? She felt the pull of the mountains, but forced her hands to keep the motorcycle steady.

The old books had pictures, drawings so real they were like looking into another time. In those, the cities looked big enough to hold tens of hundreds of people. With so many people, all working together, you could do anything! Well, here it was just her and Harissa. And maybe a few more, if this worked.

The motorcycle rode over a human skull, crushed it. Murdergirl slowed down, brought her focus back to the desert. Even if you were dead, you wouldn't want somebody crushing your skull.

The color of the desert changed. Blacker, redder, the color of what came out of you one week in a month. They rode into the shadow of a mountain, slowing to a stop before they went around the curve of its base.

She put one foot barely onto the surface of that red-black sand. Nothing. She put it down all the way. The sand crunched lightly, like any other sand in the desert. No heat came from the ground. No pain in her leg. The ground here was poison, everybody knew that. Hopefully it took a long time for it to have any effect; the Skinheads lived here all their lives, that explained why it had made them crazy.

They continued on foot. It was cool in the shade. As they rounded the mountain, a few skin horses turned their heads to look, then turned back to plucking what food they could find from the red-black sand.

Several hundred paces beyond the horses, the Skinhead farm. A pile of loose white rock marked it, twice as tall as a person. More skin horses roamed freely, dozens of them. At the edge of the farm there were cages made of seemingly whatever the Skinheads had to hand—wood, bamboo, even bones. Horse bones, human bones. Cages for the horses at night, to stop them going too far, but empty during the day.

It was better than she had hoped. Only a handful of Skinheads—five—stood in the farm. They must be the day watch, while the others slept, because the Skinheads always went out at night. But none of them seemed as if they were paying any particular attention to the area outside the camp. The poison ground was enough to keep people away, and no animals would come during the day. How long had it been since a person other than a Skinhead had come here—willingly?

They went back for the motorcycle, pushed it closer, only the sound of their feet and the rolling of the wheels on the sand. The same skin horses raised their heads and watched, a little longer this time; a motorcycle was more interesting than a person—but not much more, and they soon put their heads down again. They closed half the distance, and still not a single Skinhead looked their way.

As they came closer, the pile of rocks wasn't rocks anymore. It was a pile of bones, the Skinhead's garbage heap. They picked it clean, then tossed it on the pile. It was huge—ten persons across, three persons high. It provided perfect cover for Murdergirl and Harissa as they eased the motorcycle towards the farm. Murdergirl gagged. Even though the bones were picked clean and bleached by the desert sun, the smell of death was all around.

A plume of smoke rose in the distance, marking the burning heart of the desert at the Forge, beyond the horizon. It was a good distance, about what she'd hoped for. Long enough to be a chase for the Skinheads, but not so far that they would give up and return to their farm. Did the Forge-mates know how close they lived to these human hyenas? Or did they feel so safe in their fortress of stone that it didn't matter to them?

They were close enough now to make out the faces of individual Skinheads. Or, rather, the faces that they wore over their own. She'd thought that might have just been something they did as intimidation when they went hunting, but even here, with only other Skinheads around to see, they still kept it up. Some of the skin masks hung loose; others were tight to the wearer's faces, shrunken by constant exposure to the sun and wind. The shifting folds of the loose masks gave impressions of people she had known, people she knew still. Even her own face looked back at her. Eyes within eyes, and mouths inside mouths.

This close to the farm—sixty paces, fifty paces—the death smell was almost overpowering. It seemed to rise from the desert, as if death itself soaked that red-black sand. All day, every day, the Skinheads marinated in it. They breathed death into their lungs, wore death on their faces; their lives were death, and they brought only death to the valley.

Murdergirl raised her hand for Harissa to see, and motioned towards the farm. As planned, Harissa crept forward, staying low.

Chapter 21

Harissa would get their attention, draw them out, and Murdergirl would be waiting, ready with the motorcycle. The Skinheads, on foot, would get their skin horses and give chase, all the way to the Forge. With the Skinheads right at their entrance, surely the Forge-mates would have to respond.

Murdergirl knelt at the edge of the bone mound, keeping Harissa in sight. Even out of sunlight, the girl's aloe-coated skin shone white, as white as the bones that filled this place. Against the dark sand she stood out even more, beautiful life moving over death.

Half the distance closed, and still the Skinheads had not noticed Harissa. They barely ever looked outside of the farm. Murdergirl could hardly believe it. These unorganized savages kept the whole valley awake at night, frightened? They didn't even guard themselves. If only the valley would come together, rise up, Oasis and Forge and Garden together—even the Bones, surely even they must hate the Skinheads—they could crush the Skinheads as easily as her motorcycle rolling over a skull.

Harissa turned to Murdergirl, spread her hands out questioningly. They hadn't planned for the Skinheads simply not noticing her. She had to get their attention, though. Murdergirl cupped her hands around her face and mimicked shouting. Harissa raised her eyebrows, and Murdergirl nodded.

Murdergirl turned her attention back to the farm, watchful for any Skinhead that might surprise Harissa, an ambush, anything. The row of cages at the edge of the farm partly concealed them; from this close, she could see they weren't cages for horses, too small for that. They kept *people* in cages. What sort of person could put another human behind bars? And what kind of torment it must be for any person in those cages, knowing what awaited. The Skinheads kept people in those cages the same as you might keep a fig or a handful of dried dates in your pocket for later. But for now, they were empty. Harissa crept closer still, and raised her hands to her face, ready to shout.

Beyond Harissa, Murdergirl saw that one cage wasn't empty. A person laid in it, slumped to the side, legs bent and body curled inward, not enough room in the cage to lie flat. Their head was white. No, not quite; she squinted—their head was bandaged. And more bandages around their torso. Murdergirl stood, her legs raising her up on their own. The Skinheads had Hux. She had to stop Harissa; they had to rescue him first. Forget the plan, it could wait. The Skinheads still hadn't even looked in their direction, they could get to Hux and get him out without being seen. She took a step towards Harissa. "*Wait,*" she whispered, as loud as she dared.

"Skinheads," Harissa shouted, "fuck you!"

Five Skinheads with their death masks turned to look. Harissa's shout echoed back from the mountain.

Murdergirl ran to Harissa as the girl turned back. They met after a few strides. "New plan," Murdergirl said, pointing over Harissa's shoulder to the cage. "They've got Hux."

"What's the plan?"

Murdergirl tightened her ponytail and pulled the shotgun off her back. "Who's hungry?" she shouted, advancing on the farm. Harissa ran back to the motorcycle. Four Skinheads came towards them, past the line of cages, no sign of hesitation, like you might approach a tasty meal laid out for you. Had they never seen a shotgun before? Murdergirl's face was hard, but she smiled inside. She pulled the trigger, the shotgun roared, and one Skinhead dropped. The others stopped, looked at him. Hux stirred in his cage. She fired again, still advancing; another fell, adding his death to the countless others here. She reloaded, fired again, another Skinhead dead. The fourth turned and ran, she shot him in the back before he'd gone two steps. He fell flat on his face, arms outstretched. She emptied out the shells and reached for more from the bag at her waist.

Footsteps to her left. She whirled. The fifth Skinhead had snuck around the side of the bone pile. She pulled the trigger. Only an empty click answered.

Chapter 22

He ran at her, and Harissa leapt forward past Murdergirl, jabbing a shaft of blue metal into his throat. His eyes went wide inside the skin mask, his hands gripped the bicycle spear that hung out of him, and he pitched forward, falling onto the end of it, pushing it all the way through with the weight of his own body. He fell face-down, body twitching, twisted gurgling from his mouth as his blood and breath both came out at once, bicycle spear sticking an arm-length out the back of his neck and smeared with blood.

The first time Harissa had killed someone. No time to think about that. Murdergirl stepped on the Skinhead's neck and pulled the spear out the rest of the way, causing a sucking sound as his lungs made one last attempt at life.

"I told you I'd be useful," Harissa said. Her chest heaved, and her eyes were wide. She reached out shaking hands and took the bloody spear.

"Murdergirl?" a whisper asked. Hux moved against the edge of the cage. He stood up, slowly, back bent, head bowed. His own blood soaked the bandages on his head and chest. He gripped the bone bars with hands covered in scratches and cuts.

She placed one hand over his, the other still holding the shotgun. "It's me. We're here. We've got you."

He lifted his head. The eye not covered with bandages was swollen. He looked at her through a slit between red and purple and black. A riverbed of cracked, dry blood coated the other side of his face where it had poured from his bandaged eye.

"Murdergirl, look." Harissa pointed through the cage to the other side of the camp. Her hand still shook.

The other Skinheads had risen from sleep. They stood, watching. Forty of them, fifty, more. Fine. The shotgun had woken them, she would put them back to sleep with it. The Skinheads were naked, every one of them. But there was something wrong with them, they didn't look right. They had dark and light skin. Legs with black hair, torsos with bright blonde hair. Their naked skin wasn't their own. They wore pieces of skin, different colors—one leg too small, the other side too large—skin from different people, adults and children, women and men, the bodies of five or six people having gone into making one skin suit that they used for sleeping in. She lifted the shotgun. Nobody else was going to have to suffer through having their own *skin* worn as someone else's pajamas.

"Not now," Harissa said, and pushed the shotgun back down.

She was right. Too many Skinheads. Not enough time. Not today. She turned her attention back to Hux. The cage had no lock, no door. The bones and sticks and bamboo that formed the bars were tied at every joint with thick bundles of fiber, tied over and over, dozens of intertwined knots that would take five or ten minutes to undo.

"Step back," Murdergirl said to both of them. She raised the shotgun and placed it right against one of the joints. Hux staggered into the opposite corner and turned his face away. She pulled the trigger, and a dozen balls of shot obliterated the bone joint. Shards of bone sliced into Hux's back and legs. He flinched, but did not cry out. "Give me your hand," Murdergirl said to him. She passed the shotgun to Harissa.

Hux turned to her. His swollen, bloody face made it impossible to see what he was feeling. He held out his hand. What had they done to him? Those perfect, slender fingers. His hands were caked in blood, puffy and swollen like his eyes, and covered in tiny cuts. His little finger was turned at an angle that fingers should not be turned. She almost recoiled, but forced herself to take his hand in hers. "I've got you," she said. He gripped her hand, his muscles still powerful even after what they had done to him, and slipped through the cage's broken bones.

The Skinheads came, but not in a hurry. They watched, all of them spread out in a line, slowly advancing. The shotgun had surprised them, made them pause, but they came again.

She pulled Hux's arm over her shoulder. He was taller than her, but she gave him what support she could. "We have to move," she said. He nodded. Harissa was already on her way, shotgun in one hand and bicycle spear in the other.

Murdergirl looked back. The Skinheads still came, faster now, walking steadily, enough to match her pace. Had anyone else ever been to the Skinhead farm—anyone who came here willingly? Had anyone else ever escaped from a bone cage? It was just a novelty for the Skinheads. An inconvenience, maybe. A roasted cactus nut slipping through your fingers as you were about to eat it.

Harissa disappeared behind the bone pile.

Hux said something she couldn't hear, just air rasping through a dry windpipe. He coughed, cleared his throat.

She raised her head up towards him. "Go without me," he whispered.

Before she could respond, a rumbling growl came from the bone pile. Hux was startled, almost stumbled. She put her hand around his waist, pulled him against her. She quickened her pace, pulling him along, taking more of his weight onto her. They came around the mound of bones, around the pile of a thousand and more who'd had no chance to escape. Harissa sat on the motorcycle, hands on the rubber-coated handles, looking like it was just where she belonged. But she didn't know how to control it, and this was not the time to teach her. Murdergirl got on, taking Harissa's place. Hux hesitated, just for a second. Nobody besides her and Harissa had ridden such a beast in centuries. Murdergirl held out her hand. He took it and swung his leg over the motorcycle, pressing his body onto hers. He wrapped his arms around her, placed his bloody, broken hands against her stomach, and Harissa got on behind him.

Would the beast hold the three of them? Could it bear their weight? She twisted the handle, released the brake, and the beast roared forward. They shot out from behind the pile of bones, past the Skinheads who had been taking their time, thinking the three had no way to escape. The sight of the motorcycle startled them, causing several to skid in the sand and fall as they suddenly stopped and tried to step back. Others realized their three meals were getting away, and ran for their skin horses.

Chapter 23

Reddish-black, the sand of death sprayed out behind the wheels of the beast. Its roar was as strong as ever, but Murdergirl could feel it straining under the weight of them; she had to turn the handle farther, had to give it more power for it to go as fast as it had before.

Hux rested his head on her shoulder. He spoke, and the wind nearly tore his voice away—"Thank you," he said.

Harissa tapped Murdergirl on the shoulder before she could reply. Murdergirl looked back. Harissa jerked her thumb behind. Skinheads, a dozen and more, were close behind on their skin horses. Trailing behind them were even more, many more.

"What is it?" Hux asked.

"Skin horses. Skinheads. All of them."

Murdergirl eased off on the handle, and the beast's roar calmed.

Hux's head snapped up. "What are you doing?" he asked. Bandaged, swollen, bruised, his face was unreadable, but behind it there had to be the terror of facing being eaten alive.

"They're never getting another meal," she shouted over the wind.

The Skinheads drew closer, just three or four person-lengths behind. The sound of the galloping skin horses thundered, mingling with the steady growl of the motorcycle.

There was an explosion from behind. A small geyser of sand jetted up from the ground far ahead of them.

"He's got a gun!" Harissa shouted. Murdergirl whipped her head around. A Skinhead, grinning through his death mask, pointed a zip-pistol at them. The other Skinheads whooped. The tangled, bloody hair of their masks streamed out behind them.

Skinheads with guns? It was just as Hux had said.

He fired again, light and smoke and sound exploding from the zip-pistol. Again, the bullet missed. Shoddily made, his gun was much louder even than her shotgun, and its aim was not true.

Another shot. The bullet zipped by, closer this time—the sound boomed in her ears. Sand from the bullet impact rattled against the motorcycle's body. Even if the gun was not well made, with enough shots his aim would find its mark. How many bullets did he have? And where had the Skinheads got them from?

The Skinhead's finger pulled the trigger once more, and his skull erupted with a pink and red spray of brain and blood as his zip-pistol disintegrated in a final explosion and fired the bullet directly into his own face. His blood speckled the bodies of the nearest Skinheads. The risk of a zip-pistol—made by unskilled human hands, some small defect could cause your own death just as easily as another's. He toppled backwards and thudded to the ground, a sack of meat on the baking sand. His horse slowed and veered away from the group.

A chorus of whoops rose from the Skinheads pursuing them, cutting through the galloping hooves and the growling motorcycle. They kicked their heels in to the sides of their skin horses, urging them on towards the beast and its riders. The death of one of their own hadn't slowed them down at all. Murdergirl's stomach turned. They knew it was a guaranteed meal for them to collect later; they were probably already salivating over his tender organs.

The Forge's column of smoke rose up into the sky ahead of them, growing larger. Had the Skinheads ever been there? The Forge-mates in their stone fortress probably didn't fear the Skinheads, and the Skinheads would not fear the Forge-mates.

The explosion of a zip-pistol shot cracked again. Murdergirl instinctively ducked, and the front wheel of the motorcycle skidded before she regained control. Another shot, and another. She turned to look. More of the Skinheads—five…no, ten—aimed zip-pistols. Whoops and howls from the others spurred them on as they spurred on their galloping horses, a relentless army of the living dead in their flapping skin masks.

Murdergirl turned the handle, gave the beast more power. She felt Harissa's hand on her shoulder and she knew what the girl was telling her—keeping the chase going was important. But they couldn't stay so close. Her whole body was stiff, muscles taut and hard, joints rigid. Any moment a bullet could hit her, Harissa, Hux, the heart of the beast.

She quickly glanced over her shoulder, checking the distance. The ground erupted in front of the Skinheads, spraying geysers of sand into the air. Several skin horses collapsed, throwing their riders to the ground, before the sand cloud hid them all from view.

As the air cleared, six figures, the same color as the sand, stood in the path of the Skinheads. Too far away to see much about them, but they had to be Worms. Two leapt to opposite sides, pulling a rope out of the sand and taut between them, tripping five horses, their Skinhead riders dumped in a writhing heap. The Skinheads moved to get up, but a cloud of sand and dust exploded around them; another Worm dashed in, a bamboo spear making quick jabs into the cloud, coming out coated in blood. The skin horse herd slowed and split, flowing around the Worms, who lashed out with their sand bombs and bamboo spears, enveloping individual Skinheads and their horses in a golden cloud that they exited blinded and streaming blood. First ten Skinheads were down, and then twenty, and then the rest galloped past, leaving the Worms as quickly as they had met them, skin horse hooves beating the ground.

The Worms turned. Murdergirl felt they were looking at her, watching her, watching the progress of the beast. What did they want, and why? Why were they here, and why now? The sight of Skinheads and their zip-pistols put those thoughts out of her head, and she gave the motorcycle power.

Hoofbeats faded away as the distance between them and the Skinheads increased. The *crack, crack* of zip-pistols still sounded over the roar of the motorcycle; each one made her body try to tense itself even further. Her jaw ached from clenched teeth.

"Where are we going?" Hux asked, his pained voice barely audible. Surely he had never been out this far from the Garden before, and there were few landmarks, but it was hard to miss the smoke from the Forge as it filled the sky ahead.

Was it right to take him with them? To involve him in a plan he had no part in forming? The distant pop of a zip-pistol reminded her that she had no choice. They could have gone to the Garden, but then what? If the Skinheads came, if the Bones came with them, there would be no holding them back. She could run forever on the beast, but there would never be true safety for anyone in the Valley while these mockers of death roamed free.

By way of answer, Murdergirl nodded her head in the direction of the Forge. There was not much to say. There was what Harissa believed and what Murdergirl hoped, but that alone did not make a plan. So much of it relied on others who had even less knowledge of the situation than Hux did.

He gripped her waist in a way that she took for acceptance. If he had been involved in the plan, he would have agreed to it, he would have fought to protect the Garden. If anything, he was a part of the plan after all—their rescue of him from the Skinhead food pantry surely had tempted them to give chase.

Hux's body jerked behind her. He cried out at the same moment that the sound of the shot reached her ears.

"Hux!" Murdergirl twisted her head to see him. His dark face, contorted by a grimace, had turned the color of ash.

"I'm okay," he said, each word a ragged gasp through clenched teeth. His eyes were squeezed shut against the pain.

What about Harissa? Had she also been shot? Murdergirl couldn't see behind Hux. "Harissa?" she called.

For a moment there was no response, and then Harissa's face appeared to the side of Hux's. She put her hand out, fingers and palm bloody, and showed a little round ball of blood-dripping metal that she had taken from his back. Knowledge gained from her fifteen years at Rebecca's side.

Hux laid his head on Murdergirl's shoulder. With one hand still holding the power handle, she put her other hand up to stroke his cheek. She looked down at him, keeping one eye watching where they were going. His skin was still gray, but with the shot-ball out of his back his face relaxed a little. The roar of the motorcycle felt gentle, they had become used to it. The crackle of the zip-pistols had stopped. It was only a moment that she looked at him, perhaps less than a second, but it felt much longer. They were going to make it. The dream was real, the dream was true. She couldn't allow herself a smile, but everything that she had done, everything that she still had to do, it was all worth it. Then his eyes widened. "Look out!"

Murdergirl tore her gaze away and whipped her head around. A rock larger than the motorcycle rushed up to meet them. Murdergirl swerved, leaning the beast low to the ground, spraying sand up into the air. They hurtled past the rock, scraping their thighs against it. But they were past. And then another rock the size of a human head smashed against the front wheel of the beast. The machine bounced into the air. Murdergirl's stomach dropped, and she let off the power handle. The engine immediately quieted. They soared in the air, free, and then smashed back to the earth. The handles jerked with the impact and tore out of Murdergirl's hands, turning the motorcycle sharply and crazily to the side and dumping the three riders onto the desert sand.

Chapter 24

The earthy smell of the Forge filled her nostrils. The sand was rough against her face and hands. Rocks of all sizes were strewn about the land. Far above, black smoke from the heart of the desert drifted. Pain on the side of her face, skin scratched and torn. She heard her own breathing. Harissa coughed and spat out sand. Hux groaned. All alive. They had made it to the Forge.

There was nothing. No other sounds. Not even a crevice cricket. Sand crunched under her as she rolled over. A gentle whistling breeze that stung her cheek where the fall had scraped it.

The distant thud of a hundred hooves. Faint whoops carried on the wind. Murdergirl sat up. They might be at the Forge, but a Skinhead could cut your scalp off just as easily there as in their own camp. A zip-pistol cracked in the distance.

"Get up," she said. "Hux, Harissa, come on."

The beast was lying on its side a few steps away. She hefted it upright. Hux staggered over and climbed on. Harissa behind him. Murdergirl turned the metal. It groaned and coughed and died. Her heart pumped cold blood. The Skinheads galloped onward. "Come on," she whispered to the motorcycle. "Come on, not now. You can do this." She turned the metal again. Cough. Sputter. Skinheads close enough now to see their death masks, dried-blood scraggly hair streaming behind them.

"Come on, you motherfucking beast!" Once more, she turned the metal, and the beast roared to life, ready to fight. A shot-ball crashed into a nearby rock, shattering it. Shards of the rock clattered against the beast's metal body. Murdergirl gave it power, and they zoomed away.

Sand gave way to rock beneath them. The black-rock fortress of the Forge filled their view, and above, the burning heart of the desert billowed smoke ever upward. Small rocks littered the ground, and larger ones jutted up, many-faceted spikes threatening death. Murdergirl kept the speed lower so she could maneuver between them, turning one way and then the other.

The sound of skin horse hooves rattled louder as they also reached the rock surface. The Skinheads had followed, just as planned. Murdergirl allowed herself to hope. She took the beast to within two person-lengths of the fortress and drove it alongside. Its needle rested at thirty. The echo of its roar off the fortress wall was deafening.

She lifted her face upward and screamed. A scream from deep inside, a scream that had been waiting to come out for decades. Harissa's scream joined with hers. They screamed for their mothers, for Rebecca, for every person who had lived and died in the Valley for hundreds of years and never even known what humanity could be. Tears streamed down her face and the wind whipped them away.

Faces appeared high up, over the edge of the fortress wall. Forge-mates. One, two, ten, twenty. Murdergirl circled the motorcycle around the Forge, time after time. The Skinheads followed, a herd of hooves booming against the ground, mingling with the roar from the motorcycle, the sounds reflecting off the fortress to the larger rocks nearby and back again. Murdergirl's throat was raw, and still she screamed. They screamed for themselves. They screamed for each other. They screamed for the desert itself.

Murdergirl had kept ahead of the Skinhead horde, keeping the motorcycle just in sight of them at the curve of the fortress, but now she turned the handle and the beast jumped forward. She sped ahead of the Skinheads, racing to the front of the Forge. At the entrance, she pulled the beast up, bringing it to a skidding stop, tilted to the side with one foot on the ground.

Three Forge-mates she hadn't seen before stood in the entrance, shoulder to shoulder, completely blocking the way. Each of the trio held their wooden spear. Behind them, several others.

"The Skinheads are here!" Murdergirl shouted.

"Well," a familiar voice called from behind her, "ain't this a situation."

Chapter 25

Murdergirl turned, looking over Hux and Harissa. Hambone! Five paces away, all of the Bones stood with him among the stones before the fortress.

Hambone grinned his white grin. "I was just talking to my friends here at the Forge about where you might be," he said.

Friends? She glanced back at the Forge-mates. Their faces told her nothing.

Murdergirl kicked down the stand of the motorcycle and swung her leg off. She turned to face Hambone. "Friends? You don't have any friends in this whole Valley." She reached back for her shotgun.

"Ah," Hambone said, raising a finger. "That's just what we had been discussing. A gun from the before time. Murdergirl's gun." He looked down with a smile. "Why do you reckon they call her Murdergirl?" He looked up at the fortress, at the Forge-mates that lined the wall above the entrance. He raised one eyebrow. "Well, I'll let you draw your own conclusions."

"You gave me this name," she said.

"Hmm? What's that?" He cupped a hand around his ear.

"I said—"

"And what kind of power does a weapon like that give someone?" He called, cutting her off. He raised his hands, palm up. "The power of life, the power of death. Power that only the desert should have," he pointed at her, "and she took it. Used it to destroy the humble place I called home."

"You have guns!" Harissa shouted.

"Us?" Hambone tilted his head slightly, with what looked like an embarrassed smile. He pulled a zip-pistol out of his waistband. He shook it, and it rattled. "Poorly made, by ignorant hands." He stroked his palm over the rusty metal. "The surface is rough." He turned around and pointed it at a large rock behind him. "And the aim?" He pulled the trigger. At such close range, it was an explosion in the ears of every person there. The shot ball smashed another rock to the side and far behind the first one. Hambone turned back to face the Forge. He tossed the zip-pistol on the ground, and it fell to pieces. "We have only these wretched imitations of the past," he said. "Are they a threat to anyone? No. They are barely good for scaring off a hyena."

"That's not true," Harissa said. "And you have another! You killed Rebecca with it!"

Hux pushed past Murdergirl and turned so his back was towards the Forge. With a grunt of pain, he jerked his thumb over his shoulder at his wound. Blood soaked his clothes and had dripped all the way down his back. In a voice that he forced to be loud, he said, "This is what one of your wretched imitations did to me."

Hambone paused for a moment, mouth open slightly. Then his face formed a smile. "The Gardener, yes." His smile widened, showing his bone-white teeth. "You're not supposed to be here."

The thundering of the Skinhead horses, which had been increasing steadily, now reached a crescendo as they rounded the curve of the fortress. The Forge-mates exclaimed when the horde came into sight, and the ones lining the wall above the entrance brandished their wooden spears.

"Help us," Murdergirl said to the Forge-mates at the entrance.

"This is not our fight," one of them replied. Shamon, the guardian of the entrance.

"It is your fight! It's mine, it's ours, it's the fight of the desert. Hear me!" Where was Pig? "Pig!" she called out. "Help us!"

Shamon shook his head. "You brought this on yourself, with your weapon from the past. Just like the ones who lived before, with their weapons they destroyed themselves, they poisoned the earth, they created the Skinheads."

"And now she has brought the Skinheads to you!" Hambone interjected. "Monsters, clothed in the skin of their victims, they would eat you, me, every one of us here if they could. They would drink our blood and bathe in it."

As the Skinheads galloped closer, the Forge-mates drew back into the entrance of their fortress for the protection of the cold stone.

"Please!" Harissa screamed. She turned and faced the fortress, upturned face pleading for help. "Are you going to let them kill us?"

The Forge-mates did not respond. Hambone grinned. Wafers of ash floated through the air between them.

This wasn't how it was supposed to be. Murdergirl felt the weight of the shotgun on her back. They could escape. Perhaps she could even kill Hambone. But what about the Valley? If the Forge-mates would work with the Bones, would they also work with the Skinheads?

No.

She turned to face the onrushing Skinheads. Skin horses galloped wildly towards the three lone Gardeners. Underneath the skin masks, their riders wore expressions of delirious happiness, the pleasure of a goal nearly attained. Had there ever been a hunt like this for them before?

For this meal, she hoped they liked the taste of lead. She slung the shotgun off her back. She raised it to her shoulder. Waited. A hundred hooves and more thundered on the ground. Waited. She could see the whites of their eyes behind their masks. As the horde bore down on them, she could no longer hear the hooves. She could hear only her own breath, slow and steady.

She pulled the trigger. The shotgun kicked against her shoulder and flame leapt from the barrel. Three Skinheads at the front dropped from their horses, their bodies trampled instantly. The horses veered to the sides, and others had to pull up or turn away, opening up a fork in the river of horses. But it quickly filled with more of the skin horses.

There would not be time for many more shots. Murdergirl ejected the shells from the shotgun and loaded more into it. The Skinheads rushed towards them like a sandstorm, with a cloud of dust filling the air behind them.

"Pocket mouuuuse!" A voice shouted from behind the fortress walls. And then, at the top, a man nearly as hairy as a hyena appeared, shoving the other Forge-mates aside. Pig vaulted over the wall, landing solidly on the rock ground. In his hand he held a bicycle spear. He launched it and it sailed true, piercing the chest of a Skinhead, who looked down at it dumbly and grasped it with his hands as he toppled off his horse.

The onrushing horde of Skinheads and their horses were nearly upon them. Pig grabbed Harissa about the waist and raced for the fortress entrance. The Forge-mates parted for them, and they disappeared into the fortress.

"Come on, you hopeless bastards," Pig shouted, out of sight. "Fight them!"

Harissa was safe. There was only herself and Hux. He had said he would fight with them, and here he was. It was okay. For the desert, she only had one last thing to do. Spears from the Forge-mates rained onto the Skinheads. Some made of metal, but mostly wooden, which took them down all the same. Murdergirl turned away from the Skinhead herd towards Hambone, shotgun held low and steady.

Three or four strides away, in the relative safety of the man-sized stones, Hambone aimed his pistol at her head. Far back among the stones, Murdergirl saw movement. Glendin was there, face bloodied. Behind him, more from the Garden filled the spaces in the stones. They crept forward. One Gardener grabbed a Bone from behind, clamped a hand over his mouth, and as the Bone struggled another Gardener cracked a rock onto his head. Blood spattered them.

The Gardeners had come. The Forge would fight. But even as the Valley's future was opening up, it was too late for her. Hambone's pistol was the old one. Black and polished. With a zip-pistol, maybe he could have missed. But with this gun, machine-made, precise, true—he could not miss.

Without a word or even a look, Hux stepped in front of her as Hambone pulled the trigger. The bullet smashed into his skull. His blood splattered Murdergirl's face. His body staggered backwards against her. Instinctively, she took his hand—for the last time. Those slender fingers slipped from her grasp. Hux dropped to the ground. At the same time, a Skinhead fell from his horse and skidded along the rock, a bicycle spear through the back of his neck.

Skin horses thundered all around Murdergirl. She was in the middle of the horde. Hux's blood pooled around her feet. She screamed, and fired the shotgun towards Hambone. A skin horse took the shots and thudded to the ground, tossing its rider to his death. Hambone ducked out of sight. Murdergirl fired at the nearest Bone, and his clothes sprouted bloody holes. She dashed for the Bones. Zip-pistols fired at her. Some hit the fortress, some hit the Skinheads.

Skinheads jumped from their horses. They also went for the Bones. Whatever truce they'd had was temporary. They pounced onto the nearest Bones, ripping at their flesh with their teeth while the Bones were still alive. Whoops rose from the horde—mealtime calls. A volley of zip-pistols cracked again from the Bones. Skinheads, with blood flowing from their bodies, still came forward, eager for just one bite of steaming meat before the end. Skinhead clubs hurtled through the air, smacking into flesh and cracking against rock.

Murdergirl reloaded. She went into the rocks. The clang of metal against stone reverberated among them. Hooves clattered. *Crack.* Zip-pistols continued to fire. Around a corner, a Skinhead appeared, his teeth gory, blood dripping down the chin of the hideous mask. She smashed his face in with the butt of the shotgun, adding his own blood.

Smoke from the Forge blew through the stones, blotting out the light. She caught sight of bone-white teeth ahead, then Hambone whirled and was away, vanishing into the black smoke. A Bone stepped in front of her, started to raise his zip-pistol, and she pulled the trigger on the shotgun. His body crumpled and went to the ground, leaking blood.

A blood-smeared bicycle spear lay on the ground. Murdergirl scooped it up in her hand as another Skinhead ran towards her, and in the same movement launched it into his chest. He paused, only briefly, and redoubled his speed. She put out one boot into his stomach and tugged on the spear. It came out slickly followed by a wet gurgling from the hole, and she plunged it into the other side of his chest. A shove with the boot, and he fell back, popping the spear up to clang on the ground beside him, and a fountain of blood spurted from his mouth. His lips moved behind his bloody mask, and he spoke in a rattling, rasping whisper. Murdergirl stomped on his mouth. The bones of his face crunched under her foot, and he was silent.

Chapter 26

An explosion. A feeling like a punch to the back. Murdergirl spun around. The chaos of the battle was all around, and shots continued to fire. A Bone stood directly in front, his smoking zip-pistol aimed at her. Murderboy. A warm, wet flowing down her back. Her own blood. At the front, more blood. It had gone straight through. Her breath only came halfway—her lung was punctured. She felt the blood rise in her throat. This was how Murderboy planned to get his name back. They had both joined the Bones at the same time. She had been looking for something different, some kind of hope. Had he been looking for this very moment?

Behind Murderboy, Hambone stood. Fear in his face, no smile. And then he saw the blood on her tattered vest. His smile returned.

One shell left in the shotgun. It was all she needed.

She tossed the shotgun up in the air towards Murderboy and dashed forward. His eyes went wide, and he put his hands up to defend himself. The shotgun came down, she grabbed it out of the air and slung it with all her strength into the side of his head. His hands dropped, and he dropped. She kicked him in the face on the ground. One less Bone for the Valley to worry about.

She moved to raise the shotgun, but Hambone raised his own pistol first. Without the oxygen her muscles needed, she was slow. This time, there was nobody around to save her, nobody to take the bullet for her. Hux was dead. This fucking monster had killed him. Hambone had left behind whatever made him human, he was as bad as the Skinheads. He didn't consume the flesh, but it didn't matter. It made him worse. He didn't even kill to eat, like an animal did or like the Skinheads did, he killed because he liked it.

Murdergirl's body shook from the exertion of the battle. Even though he could shoot first, she raised her shotgun.

Hambone's smile broadened, showing teeth and gums. "My, my," he said. "Look at you. Look at how you've killed. How many has it been? Mmm. Might be a hundred by now. Davey told me from the beginning you shouldn't be a Bone, but look at you now. I knew." He lowered his gun. "Come back to us. Let's do this together." He gestured in a circle with the tip of the pistol. "The whole Valley can be ours. Think of it! No more killing, just peace. Peace that we will hold tight in our own hands."

"Hear this." Murdergirl pulled the trigger once more. The shotgun roared and filled his body with metal. He fell to his knees. His gun dropped from his hand, clattered to the ground.

Fear rushed back to his face. Murdergirl dropped the shotgun. She strode towards him. Took his head in both hands and smashed her knee into his face. He toppled backwards with a groan.

Hambone lay on his back. His blood seeped out from underneath his body and trickled from his nose down his cheeks. He moaned with pain, then laughed sharply, coughed and winced. Blood coated his white teeth as he smiled again.

"I knew you could be it," he said.

She kicked him in the head. He tried to move away, using his hands to slide a few inches along the cold ground.

A smear of blood remained where he had been. One of his eyes was solid red where Murdergirl's boot had made contact.

He coughed again and spat up blood. "I couldn't do it." He sighed. "So many times, I had the..." he sucked in a ragged breath "...had the chance to kill you."

"You expect me to be grateful?" She stomped on his stomach, where several holes pumped bright blood up to meet the fresh air. Hambone groaned deeply and brought his hands up to her ankle. His hands were barely there, like being gripped by a ghost. Then they slipped away.

Hambone's one good eye was unfocused. He looked at her, looked through her.

"Grateful? It doesn't matter," he whispered. "You are what I made you." He grinned his bloody-white grin. "*Murdergirl.*"

She knelt with one knee pressed into his chest. His breath was a thin, labored wheeze under her weight. She scooped up his gun from the ground, put the barrel against his temple, and pulled the trigger. Brains, blood, and bone exploded out the other side of his head.

His eyes saw nothing, but his smile was still there. She screamed at his shattered face. A weak scream, her own body damaged from the fight, one lung barely functioning. Her scream ended in a sob. All of this, he had made her do it. She flipped the pistol around and smashed the back of it into his face. Blood spattered up onto her. Onto her chest, onto her face. Over and over, with all of her fading strength, she rammed the chunk of death metal into his face until there was nothing left but a dark and gory pit of flesh and bone. No eyes, no nose, especially no fucking smiling mouth. Her tears rained down to mix with his blood. How many people had died? How many had she killed? She fired the pistol into his corpse. The gunshot was the only sound other than her sobs. Again, she fired. She pulled the trigger, filled him with bullets. *Click, click, click, click, click.* There was nothing left. Nothing left in the gun, nothing left in her. She let it fall. She looked at her hands. Coated with blood. Hambone's. Her own. Skinheads and Bones. The blood of so many people. What had she become?

Murdergirl beat her fists into Hambone's lifeless body. Wet thuds against his bloody chest. She tore at his chest with her nails, through his ripped shirt. She gouged out his flesh with her fingers. It was done. Nothing more could be done. He could not be killed further. She could not be saved. You couldn't go back.

The blows came slower. Finally, she rested, palms down, on Hambone. Her muscles had nothing left in them. She drew in a breath, it was cold and raw on her throat, and flame in her lungs.

Her arms gave out and she collapsed forward, lying prone partly on top of Hambone. Tried to push herself back up; her muscles wouldn't do it. Blood leaked from her body. She coughed out a bloody sob and let her eyes close.

She heard footsteps. "Under the arm," a man's voice said. Pig. She could hear him, couldn't see him. They lifted her. Carried her out of the rocks, away from all the death. They carried her over the battlefield, towards the fortress.

Her head lolled to the side, and her eyes opened. Bodies as far as she could see. The dead eyes of a hundred corpses watched her.

They jerked, dropped her on the ground. She fell next to the body of a dead Forge-mate, face to face. His mouth was open in fear, face twisted with the pain of his last moment.

"Careful!" Pig hissed. "Watch where you step."

With soft hands, they picked her up again. As they raised her, she saw a Skinhead nearby, dead, sat with his back against a horse. His dead eyes saw right into her. He was smiling. Laughing.

Bodies coated the hard ground like moss on a rock. How many were dead because of her? Forge-mates, Skinheads and their skin horses, Bones, Gardeners. The ones carrying her moved slowly, picking their way among the death.

A fresh breeze blew away the smoke from the Forge. She breathed. The cool, clear, desert air. The sun gently touched the back of her neck. She had done it. No matter the cost, she had done it. They were free.

Chapter 27

Murdergirl stepped out of the tent into the sunlight, shielding her eyes with her hand. Her other hand felt her chest through her vest. A scar that would always remain, but the pain was now only a memory.

Harissa ran through the sand to meet her. "Murdergirl, you're up!"

Murdergirl smiled and folded her arms around the girl. "What are you so excited about?"

"Come and see! Pig says it's almost ready."

Murdergirl and Harissa walked through the desert, over dunes where Murdergirl had walked before, where Harissa had led her. So much had happened since then. She heard the shrieks of the dying. She stopped and turned her head away, closed her eyes. The sobbing and screams of a thousand people. Her breath caught in her throat.

"Murdergirl?" Harissa put out a hand on her shoulder. "Are you okay?"

Murdergirl opened her eyes and exhaled sharply. The screams were gone; wind whistled in her ears. She smiled a half-smile. "Just the wound," she said, touching her fingertips to her chest.

Harissa put her palm over Murdergirl's hand. "It's more than that, isn't it? You're different."

Murdergirl sighed. "You're starting to remind me of Hux."

"I'm different, too," Harissa said. Her eyes were suddenly serious. Dark. Far away.

She nodded. "I know. But come on. What would Rebecca say?"

"'Every day is a new terror'?" Harissa said, a small smile returning to her face.

Murdergirl snorted a laugh. "How about 'get busy living in the desert, or get busy dying in the desert'? Let's go see what they're up to."

They crested a dune. A large group of people filled the little valley before them as well as up the face of the next dune. Gardeners, Forge-mates, people of the Oasis. Even a former Skinhead was there; a woman with long, tangled red hair, skin white as bone from a lifetime under its grisly clothing that had now been replaced by a simple woven cloak. Nobody was within twenty steps of her, and she kept her eyes down.

A small chasm lay open at the top of the dune. People stood all around the edge of it, hard at work. They had cleared the sand away from the ground, and it lay around in vast piles, exposing the rock underneath. Their tools were bicycle spears with hunks of rocks from the Forge welded onto their tops, and with these they struck at the rock beneath them with resounding *clangs*. Pig stood among them, sweat streaming down his hairy body.

"Murdergirl!" he called. "Pocket mouse!" He waved them over and tossed his tool on a pile of sand.

With the back of his forearm, Pig wiped his brow. "I'm glad you could make it," he said to Murdergirl. He tilted his head to the hole in the ground, which was barely big enough for a child to fit. The sound of the river below poured up from the hole. "Only a few more minutes," he said.

Clang. Clang.

All around the hole, a circular channel two person-lengths across had been cut deep into the rock. They had fully mined through parts of the channel, and the bright blue of the cave below shone out. Six people worked on one end of the circle, hammering away.

Clang. Murdergirl flinched, and her arm moved on its own towards the shotgun strapped to her back. In her mind, skin horses galloped past, hooves clanging on the stony ground. She forced her arm to stop, and brought it down to her side. She closed her eyes. Blood splattered on her face. Gunshots all around. A soft hand on her shoulder brought her back. Her eyes opened, and she met Harissa's gaze. She blew out her breath.

A rumbling, creaking sound from the ground. "Step back!" Pig called out. The miners stopped, scrambling back from the channel they had dug. The circle of stone shifted downwards. For a moment, it rested. Then it dropped, falling to the floor of the cave far below. A thunderous crash as it smashed into the ground and shattered. A cheer from all present.

Pig laughed and clapped Murdergirl on the back. "Will you be the first?" he asked. He pointed to where a thick post, weighted with bags of sand, stood nearby. A pile of tightly braided bamboo rope lay next to it. Murdergirl hesitated.

"It's because of you that we could do this," Pig said. He looked into her eyes, searching them. Could he know what it had cost? "Thank you," he said. He held out his hand, and she took it. He gently guided her to the post. She picked up one end of the rope pile and tossed it into the hole. It unfurled itself into a braided ladder.

Another rope was also attached to the post, and Pig looped it around Murdergirl's waist. On a distant dune, she saw a dozen Worms watching. Did anyone else see them? But then she was descending the ladder. Faces appeared around the hole, shrinking as she climbed down.

The sound of the river rushing past filled the cave, filled her ears. Somehow, it was quiet. The luminescent blue light was still dark. Her body relaxed, which was when she realized her muscles had been tight for months.

She sat on a rock near the cave wall. She watched the river. There was enough water for everyone in the Valley, always and forever. It had been here before any of them were alive, before Rebecca, before Rebecca's mother, and her mother's mother. They only had to reach out and grasp it. And now they had. She breathed. Down here, the air was cold in her lungs. She closed her eyes. There was only the river, the darkness, and her.

Someone touched her shoulder. She opened her eyes. Harissa sat next to her. The others came down the ladder, until there were dozens of people in the cave. Too many people. Some carried their tools, rock fused to metal—those could smash someone's face in, crush their bones. The river flowed with blood. Her breath quickened. The roar that filled her ears—a herd of horses? Mixed with the gurgling breaths of lungs filled with blood? Her shoulders ached, muscles tense and ready for a fight.

For a moment, she'd had peace. Her eyes burned. Tears overflowed them and dropped down her cheeks. Harissa laid her head on Murdergirl's shoulder; the girl's tears wet her vest. Murdergirl leaned her head against Harissa's. She wanted to close her eyes, but she couldn't. The others laughed, played, admired their work, made plans.

Chapter 28

Murdergirl tightened the straps holding bags across the freshly refueled motorcycle. They were stuffed with dried fruit and gallons of water. Her shotgun was slung across her back. A bag of shells at her hip.

"Are you sure you can't stay?" Glendin asked.

She looked at the older man. She shook her head, and he nodded. His bald head bore its own scars from the battle to free the Valley, he understood her in some way.

Pig stepped forward, put his hand on her shoulder and looked into her eyes, brow furrowed. "Thank you," he said.

No response was needed. They heard each other.

"And take care of this little mouse," he said, completely enclosing Harissa in a hug. Did his lower lip tremble? "She's only small. Used to keep her in my pocket." He turned away his eyes, looking into the mountains. "Like a kangaroo."

Harissa laughed and wriggled out of the hug. "There's no such thing as a kangaroo," she said. Together, she and Murdergirl mounted the motorcycle. Murdergirl knocked the stand up, turned the metal, gave it power. The beast roared, ready for adventure.

They left the Garden behind, quickly. Murdergirl didn't look back, she couldn't. Glendin and Pig would take care of it.

Harissa and Murdergirl rode silently. They passed the Tomb Tree. Then mountains came up ahead, and the sand turned dark, the death-red of the former Skinhead camp.

Without the Bones, without the Skinheads, the people of the Valley could come together and breathe. They could live.

A path wound its way through the trees and up. Murdergirl steered the beast towards it. Into the mountains. Would it help? Could it? Wherever she went, she would still be Murdergirl.

THE END

Jonathan-David Jackson was born in North Carolina, raised in Tennessee, and now lives in England with his wife, author Emma Jackson. He has petted at least one hundred cats, including the one above. His mother wanted a picture of him printed here.

Other books by Jonathan-David Jackson

Dark Humor Trilogy

The Quest for Juice

The Quest for Truth

The Quest for Nothing in Particular

Supernatural Thriller

Faith of the Forsaken

Gentle Postapocalyptic Dark Humor

Not Quite the End of the World

A Brief Note from the Author

Hi! Thanks for reading my book. Since you made it to the end, I hope that means you enjoyed it. If you did, please leave a review wherever you bought it from, or at your preferred book review place. I'm an independent author, and reviews really help me to reach new readers.

To get semi-regular updates on what I'm writing next, hear about what else is going in my life and maybe even see a couple of pictures of things, sign up for my newsletter at jonathandavidjacksonwrites.com/news

(Version 9.05.24)

www.ingramcontent.com/pod-product-compliance
Lightning Source LLC
LaVergne TN
LVHW091322150826
845673LV00006B/1737

* 9 7 8 1 9 1 5 9 2 3 5 4 7 *

CATALOGUE

DES

TABLEAUX ANCIENS

DES ÉCOLES FRANÇAISE, HOLLANDAISE ET FLAMANDE

TROIS ŒUVRES DE BOILLY

BEAUX PORTRAITS DE L'ÉCOLE FRANÇAISE

OBJETS D'ART ET D'AMEUBLEMENT

Grande statue d'Adam en marbre blanc, attribuée à Lombardo
Sculptures en ivoire — Jolie pendule du XVIe siècle en cuivre gravé et doré
Grand landier en fer — Quelques armes
Faïences de Nevers et de Rouen — Verrerie de Venise
Belles porcelaines de Sèvres, de Saxe et de Chine
Beaux bras et beaux candélabres du temps de Louis XVI
Lustre garni de cristaux de roche
Miroir métallique du XVIe siècle avec cadre en bois sculpté
Meubles et panneaux en bois sculpté du XVIe siècle
Grand meuble en bois noir — Meuble en bois de fer sculpté
Étoffes et tapisseries

DONT LA VENTE AURA LIEU

HOTEL DROUOT, SALLE N° 8

Le Jeudi 1er Mars 1883, à 2 heures

COMMISSAIRE-PRISEUR

Me PAUL CHEVALLIER, successeur de Me CHARLES PILLET
10, rue Grange-Batelière, 10

EXPERTS

POUR LES OBJETS D'ART	POUR LES TABLEAUX
M. CH. MANNHEIM	M. CHARLES GEORGE
7, rue Saint-Georges, 7	12, rue Laffitte, 12

EXPOSITION PUBLIQUE : le Mercredi 28 Février 1883
De une heure à cinq heures.

CONDITIONS DE LA VENTE

Elle sera faite au comptant.

Les adjudicataires payeront *cinq pour cent* en sus des enchères.

L'exposition mettant le public à même de se rendre compte de l'état des objets, aucune réclamation ne sera admise une fois l'adjudication prononcée.

On commencera la vacation par les tableaux.

Paris. — Imprimerie de l'Art, J. Rouam, imprimeur-éditeur,
41, rue de la Victoire.

TABLEAUX

BACKHUYSEN

(LUDOLF)

1 — *Une Plage.*

Trois marchands de poisson, dont deux assis, se reposent sur la plage.

A droite, des pêcheurs déchargent leurs bateaux.

Toile. Haut., 31 cent.; larg, 41 cent.

BERKHEYDEN

(GERRIT)

2 — *La Place de la cathédrale, à Harlem.*

La vue est prise à côté de la cathédrale ; de nombreuses figures : promeneurs, marchands de poisson et de volaille, etc., animent la place au fond de laquelle on aperçoit l'hôtel de ville.

Signé et daté.

Toile. Haut., 56 cent.; larg., 48 cent.

BOILLY

(LOUIS-LÉOPOLD)

3 — *La Cuisinière.*

Elle est assise, tenant une bassine de cuivre sur ses genoux; près d'elle, sur une table à tréteaux, sont pêle-mêle des choux, du pain, un pot de beurre, une cage et diverses poteries; quantité d'ustensiles de ménage jonchent le sol.

Beau tableau signé et daté 1788.

Toile. Haut., 61 cent.; larg., 54 cent.

BOILLY

4 — *Le Souper fin.*

Un jouvenceau, le verre en main, est attablé auprès d'une coquette au regard langoureux. Il paraît également sensible aux avances de la dame et aux agaceries d'une jeune et jolie servante placée derrière le fauteuil de sa maîtresse.

Sur le piédestal d'un groupe de bacchantes, on lit :

Bacchus, l'Amour et la Folie
Sont faits pour se donner les mains.
Eux seuls soulageans les humains
Du pesant fardeau de la vie.

Toile. Haut., 65 cent.; larg., 53 cent.

BOILLY

5 — *La Leçon de musique.*

Après le duo, le maître de musique, un jeune homme en habit rouge, épris des charmes de son élève, une jeune et jolie personne en robe de satin blanc, l'a saisie par la taille et tente de lui ravir un baiser. Celle-ci ne paraît se défendre que faiblement.

Au fond, une soubrette épie la scène par une porte vitrée.

A terre, le pupitre renversé et des cahiers de musique.

Toile. Haut., 40 cent.; larg., 31 cent.

BREUGHEL

6 — *Vue d'un village au bord de la mer.*

Sur la gauche, des paysans stationnent près d'une auberge et regardent venir un carrosse attelé de trois chevaux. Au fond, la mer, sillonnée de barques de pêcheurs.

Bois. Haut., 18 cent.; larg., 24 cent.

DE TROY

(Attribué à JEAN-FRANÇOIS)

7 — *Le Repas.*

Sur la terrasse d'un château, sept joyeux convives sont attablés, dégustant les vins du dessert.

Toile. Haut., 60 cent.; larg., 92 cent.

FRAGONARD

(H.)

(?)

8 — *Le Bonheur domestique.*

Dans un intérieur rustique, une jeune femme en toilette de satin jaune et blanc est venue visiter la nombreuse famille d'un fermier et caresse le plus jeune des enfants.

Toile. Haut., 37 cent.; larg., 45 cent.

GRIMOU

9 — *Portrait d'homme.*

Vu à mi-jambes de trois quarts à droite, en costume noir, la main droite appuyée sur la hanche.

Toile. Haut., 1 m. 25 cent.; larg., 95 cent.

GRIMOU

10 — *Portrait d'un acteur.*

Il est représenté assis, jouant de la vielle.

Toile. Haut., 1 m. 25 cent.; larg., 95 cent.

HACKERT

(PHILIPPE)

11 — *Le Repos des bergers.*

Trois bergères et un pâtre, agenouillé devant elles, se reposent auprès d'un temple circulaire ombragé de grands arbres.

Signé et daté 1762.

Toile. Haut., 69 cent.; larg., 83 cent.

HOUEL

12 — *Le Retour à la ferme.*

Petite gouache ovale.

Haut., 17 cent.; larg., 13 cent.

KEYSER

(THÉODORE DE)

(?)

13 — *Portrait de femme.*

Dame âgée, en buste, de trois quarts, vêtement de soie noire, coiffe de même couleur, fraise autour du cou.

Bois. Haut., 16 cent.; larg., 13 cent.

LAJOUE

(JACQUES)

14 — *Port de mer.*

Près d'un pont, sur un quai orné d'un obélisque avec fontaine, d'une tour et d'un temple circulaire, trois personnages assistent au départ d'une galère ; des portefaix chargent des ballots sur un traîneau attelé d'un cheval blanc.

Signé à droite.

Toile. Haut., 51 cent.; larg., 76 cent.

LANTARA

(SIMON-MATHURIN)

15 — *Tempête en mer.*

La foudre sillonne les nues et on aperçoit au loin plusieurs vaisseaux battus par la tempête. A gauche se dressent d'énormes rochers au pied desquels l'artiste a tracé sa signature.

Bois. Haut., 33 cent.; larg., 41 cent.

LINGELBACH

(JAN)

16 — *La Visite au port.*

Un seigneur et sa dame viennent de débarquer sur un quai; deux portefaix chargent un ballot sur un traîneau attelé d'un cheval blanc; à droite, groupe de mariniers au repos.

Signé à droite sur une malle : *J. Lingelbach.*

Bois. Haut., 34 cent.; larg., 45 cent.

LOO

(CARLE VAN)

17 — *Portraits de Louis XVI jeune et de Marie-Antoinette.*

Deux pendants.

La reine à mi-jambe de face, en riche costume bleu brodé d'or, à manches de dentelles, diamants dans les cheveux, la main droite posée sur un manteau d'hermine.

Devant elle, la couronne royale sur un coussin rouge.

Le roi, revêtu de la cuirasse, portant le cordon de l'ordre du Saint-Esprit, la main gauche sur la hanche et la droite appuyée sur un bâton de commandement.

Toile. Haut., 1 m. 25 cent.; larg., 1 mètre.

LOO

(LOUIS-MICHEL VAN)

18 — *Portrait de jeune fille.*

Souriante, vue de trois quarts à mi-corps;

elle porte un charmant costume à la mode orientale, robe de soie rayée et manteau de velours rose, bordé d'hermine. Une aigrette et deux rangs de perles ornent ses cheveux qui sont relevés et poudrés.

Signé en toutes lettres et daté de 1766.

Toile. Haut., 72 cent.; larg., 58 cent.

LUTHERBURG

19 — *Moutons au repos.*

Près d'un abri couvert de chaume, plusieurs moutons se reposent. Un petit pâtre dort, couché sur le gazon.

Toile. Haut., 32 cent.; larg., 40 cent.

MALLET

20 — *Scène de corps de garde.*

Toile. Haut., 21 cent.; larg., 16 cent.

MEULEN

(F. VAN DER)

21 — *Le Convoi de prisonniers.*

Toile. Haut., 73 cent.; larg., 94 cent.

MOLYN

(PETER)

22 — *L'Abreuvoir.*

Des vaches viennent s'abreuver dans une mare, en avant d'un vieux castel environné d'arbres.

Signé et daté 1642.

Bois. Diam., 51 cent.

NEER

(AART VAN DER)

23 — *Effet de lune.*

La lune apparaît dans un ciel nuageux et se reflète dans les eaux d'un canal bordé d'arbres et d'habitations.

Au premier plan, deux villageois conversent sur un chemin à l'entrée d'un bois. Des vaches sont disséminées dans la prairie.

Toile. Haut., 40 cent.; larg., 53 cent.

POEL

(E. VAN DER)

24 — *La Plage de Scheveningen.*

De nombreux groupes de pêcheurs et de marchands de poisson sont disséminés sur la plage; à droite, le clocher de l'église et les toits des maisons se dressent au-dessus des dunes.

Bois. Haut., 40 cent.; larg., 61 cent.

POURBUS

dit LE JEUNE

(Attribué à FRANÇOIS)

25 — *Portrait d'enfant.*

En pied, costumé de soie noire avec fraise au cou ; il tient un petit cheval par la bride. A ses pieds est couché un chien.

Dans le haut du tableau, un blason et la date 1618.

Bois. Haut., 1 m. 10 cent.; larg., 82 cent.

PRINS

(JEAN-HUBERT)

26 — *Canal de Hollande.*

Bestiaux paissant dans un pré sur la droite, à gauche une maison entourée d'arbres, au fond un pont relie les deux berges.

Bois. Haut., 28 cent.; larg., 40 cent.

RICCI

(SÉBASTIEN)

27 — *Esquisse terminée pour plafond.*

Allégorie religieuse.

Toile carrée, 1 m. 22 cent.

RUYSDAEL

(École de J.)

28 — *Paysage des environs de Harlem.*

Bois. Haut., 25 cent.; larg., 34 cent.

SENAVE

(?)

29 — *La Lessiveuse.*

Une jeune villageoise savonne du linge dans

un baquet et cause avec une petite fille qui charge une hotte.

A terre, un chaudron, des œufs, des légumes et divers ustensiles de ménage. A droite, un monogramme.

Bois. Haut., 13 cent.; larg., 19 cent.

SMITS

(de Middelbourg)

30 — *Le Coup de canon.*

Marine.

Toile. Haut., 52 cent.; larg., 62 cent.

TAUNAY

31 — *Le Messager de la paix.*

Une branche d'olivier à la main, un cavalier montant un cheval blanc annonce aux villageois qui l'environnent que la guerre est terminée, nouvelle qu'ils accueillent en manifestant leur allégresse.

Importante composition dans laquelle on compte plus de vingt-cinq personnages, des chevaux, des chiens, des poules, etc.

Toile. Haut., 40 cent.; larg., 60 cent.

THÉAULON

(ÉTIENNE)

32 — *Les Œufs cassés.*

Une jeune fille, assise par terre dans un cellier, contemple, toute éplorée, un panier d'œufs renversé à ses pieds, tandis que l'auteur du dégât, un jeune villageois, s'esquive en souriant.

Signé en toutes lettres et daté de 1777.

Toile. Haut., 46 cent.; larg., 37 cent.

TOURNIÈRES

(?)

33 — *Portrait de jeune femme.*

Vue à mi-corps, appuyée sur une balustrade, elle caresse un petit chien.

Très beau cadre ancien en bois sculpté.

Toile. Haut., 80 cent.; larg., 65 cent.

VALLIN

34 — *Les Baigneuses.*

Une dizaine de jeunes femmes se livrent au plaisir du bain dans une rivière encaissée de rochers.

Signé et daté 1793.

Toile. Haut., 66 cent.; larg., 91 cent.

VELDE

(ADRIEN VAN DER)

35 — *Pâturage.*

Un pâtre conduit deux vaches et plusieurs moutons sur une route bordée d'arbres.

Bois. Haut., 14 cent.; larg., 18 cent.

VIGÉE-LEBRUN

(Attribué à Mme)

36 — *Portrait de Marie-Joséphine-Louise, Princesse de Savoie.*

Représentée en buste, en peignoir blanc et cheveux poudrés.

Toile ovale. Haut., 63 cent.; larg., 53 cent.

WATTEAU

(ANTOINE)

37 — *Le Singe chasseur.*

Motif d'ornementation sur fond doré, provenant d'un panneau de chaise à porteurs.

Bois. Haut., 25 cent.; larg., 29 cent.

WATTEAU

(ÉCOLE DE)

38 — *Scène de la comédie italienne.*

Trois personnages.

Toile. Haut., 75 cent.; larg., 52 cent.

WATTEAU

(DE LILLE)

39 — *Les Adieux des gardes.*

Le régiment est déjà en marche, plusieurs gardes attardés font leurs adieux à leurs maîtresses.

Cette charmante esquisse a été aussi attribuée à G. Morland.

Bois. Haut., 22 cent.; larg., 34 cent.

WEENIX

(JEAN-BAPTISTE)

40 — *Gibier sous la garde d'un chien.*

Une perdrix, un geai, un bouvreuil et autres petits oiseaux jetés à terre auprès d'une biche, d'un fusil et d'une poudrière, le tout sous la garde d'un chien blanc taché de noir, assis au pied d'un grand arbre.

Au second plan, des cavaliers précédés d'une meute poursuivent un cerf.

Toile. Haut., 52 cent.; larg., 48 cent.

WYNTRACK

41 — *Le Ruisseau.*

Un petit ruisseau baigne le pied d'un monticule sablonneux, vivement éclairé, et sillonné par un chemin creux sur lequel sont échelonnés des paysans.

Bois. Haut., 39 cent.; larg., 49 cent.

ÉCOLE FRANÇAISE

42 — *Portrait d'un commandant d'armée.*

Vu à mi-jambes, revêtu d'une armure, une main sur la hanche, l'autre appuyée sur un casque placé sur une table.

Beau cadre Régence en bois sculpté et doré.

Toile. Haut., 1 m. 28 cent.; larg., 92 cent.

ÉCOLE FRANÇAISE

(XVIIIe SIÈCLE)

43 — *Quatre panneaux décoratifs.*

Représentant des fleurs et des fruits.

Toile. Haut., 1 m. 82 cent.; larg., 62 cent.

ÉCOLE FRANÇAISE

(XVIIIe SIÈCLE)

44 — *Panneau en largeur.*

Représentant des guirlandes de feuilles, de fleurs et des couronnes de laurier entrelacées.

Toile. Haut., 67 cent.; larg., 1 m. 62 cent.

DÉSIGNATION DES OBJETS D'ART

45 — Marbre blanc. — Statue d'Adam, grandeur nature, attribuée à Lombardo. — Elle provient de la collection de Madame la duchesse de Berry.

46 — Jolie petite pendule carrée, en cuivre finement gravé et doré, décorée de médaillons de personnages, de figurines et d'ornements, et portant sur une de ses faces les armes de France et de Pologne entourées du cordon de l'ordre du Saint-Esprit. La couronne royale placée au-dessus des armoiries porte la devise suivante : *Manet . Ultima . Coelo*. Le couvre-timbre en forme de campanile est découpé à jour et les angles supérieurs sont ornés de vases. La base de la pièce porte à l'intérieur le nom de : *Matieu Bachelet*.

47 — Grand landier en fer forgé et découpé garni de ses potences et de ses chaînes. Dans le haut, une fleur de lis découpée. XVIe siècle.

48 — Grande fourche à bois en fer gravé, à tige à double balustre et rosaces découpées à jour. Travail vénitien du XVIe siècle.

49 — Petit cheval debout en bronze, sur socle en marbre. XVIe siècle.

50 — Brasero en cuivre rouge avec couvercle découpé et poignées en cuivre jaune.

51 — Grille en fer forgé, à quadrilobes et pointes formant rosaces. XVIe siècle.

52 — Lot de quelques ornements et de figurines-appliques en cuivre ciselé, gravé et découpé, tels que : armoiries des Médicis, poignée de tiroir et figurines-appliques en costumes du XVIe siècle.

53 — Plaque centrale d'un triptyque d'ivoire, sculptée en bas-relief et représentant le Christ en croix entre saint Jean et Madeleine. Cette scène est placée sous un arceau à plein cintre découpé à jour. XIIIe siècle.

54 — Coffre-fort oblong en fer gravé à l'eau-forte, à figures et ornements. Travail allemand du XVIe siècle.

55 — Batterie de fusil à pierre en fer ciselé, à figures et ornements. XVIIIe siècle.

56 — Plaque rectangulaire en ivoire sculpté en bas-relief à figures et ornements dans le goût des plaques de l'époque consulaire.

57 — Épée à poignée et garde à branches verticales en acier ciselé à ornements et fusée repercée à jour. XVIIe siècle.

58 — Coffret carré et à contours en écaille, posée d'or à paysages et ornements du temps de Louis XIV. Il contient cinq flacons en cristal avec bouchons en or ciselé.

59 — Amorçoir de forme ovoïde en bois sculpté en bas-relief et représentant le Jugement de Pâris.

60 — Beau sabre indien à longue lame et poignée richement damasquinées d'or.

61 — Lance de même travail à double pointe.

62 — Deux pièces : petit couteau japonais à fourreau laqué et couteau de chasse garni en cuivre doré.

63 — Brûle-parfums chinois en bronze, formé d'une chimère debout sur laquelle un personnage est assis. Travail ancien.

64 — Deux flambeaux formés chacun d'un personnage debout en bronze. Ancien travail chinois.

65 — Curieuse pendule en fer avec cadran de cuivre et mouvement à grande sonnerie, sur socle en bois noïr.

66 — Deux candélabres en fer forgé à trois lumières, ornés chacun d'un dragon.

67 — Deux jardinières de forme sphérique en bronze, à ouverture large, décorées d'ornements en relief.

68 — Trois petits dessins chinois sur papier, représentant des sujets familiers très délicatement traités. Dans un cadre en bois sculpté.

VERRERIE DE VENISE

69 — Grand vase porte-fleurs en verre de Venise incolore, à trois anses et à panse piriforme garnie de six goulots. Les anses en S sont garnies d'ornements travaillés à la pince.

70 — Vase de forme analogue à celui qui précède, sans goulots. La panse de celui-ci est ornée de mascarons et de mufles de lion en relief, conservant des traces de dorure.

71 — Verre de Venise à coupe évasée incolore, sur pied à balustre garni de deux ailerons en verre bleu et travaillés à la pince.

72 — Verre de Venise analogue à celui qui précède, à coupe large.

73 — Petit verre de Venise à coupe incolore ornée de godrons et de trois petites anses en verre bleu.

74 — Deux burettes en verre de Venise chevronnées d'émail blanc et à filets bleus en relief.

75 — Deux pièces en verre de Venise à filets d'émail blanc croisés; vase porte-fleur et gobelet sur pied bas et à bord évasé.

76 — Cinq petites pièces en verre de Venise incolore dont deux rehaussées de filets d'émail bleu.

FAIENCES

77 — Grande et belle buire de forme antique, en ancienne faïence de Nevers à décor bleu, de style chinois et à lambrequins. Elle est montée sur un pied rocaille en bronze

78 — Grande et belle coupe ronde à deux anses et à couvercle en ancienne faïence de Rouen, décor polychrome *à la double corne.*

79 — Grand plat oblong à angles coupés, en ancienne faïence de Sinceny, décor polychrome : corbeille de fleurs au centre, ornements et festons de fleurs au marli.

80 — Deux plateaux octogones sur piédouche en ancienne faïence de Rouen, à décor bleu.

81 — Boîte à épices de forme oblongue, en ancienne faïence de Rouen, décor polychrome à fleurs.

82 — Boîte à épices de forme analogue, en ancienne faïence de Sinceny, décor polychrome à fleurs et ornements.

83 — Amphore antique en terre cuite.

84 — Flacon carré en grès à fond bleu et médaillons armoiries en relief émaillés gris. XVIe siècle.

PORCELAINES DE SÈVRES

85 — Jolie pendule, formée d'un vase ovoïde en porcelaine tendre de Sèvres, fond gros bleu et ornements rapportés en or frappé et émaillé, attribués à Cotteau. Le cadran tournant est placé à la partie supérieure du vase et il est surmonté d'un couvercle de même travail que le vase. La garniture est en bronze ciselé et doré au mat. Elle provient de la collection Barker.

86 — Huit assiettes en ancienne porcelaine de Sèvres pâte tendre, décorées de jetés de fleurs et bord à filet bleu.

87 — Écuelle ronde à deux anses avec plateau oblong en vieux Sèvres pâte tendre, à bords décorés de branches de fleurs en camaïeu bleu et fond jaune couvert de jetés de roses et de pensées.

88 — Tasse et soucoupe en vieux Sèvres pâte tendre, fond bleu d'eau et médaillons de fleurs encadrés d'or.

89 — Théière de forme ovoïde en vieux Sèvres pâte tendre fond bleu turquoise et décorée de coquilles bleu foncé et rehaussées de dorure.

90 — Compotier en vieux Sèvres pâte tendre, à ornements gaufrés et jetés de fleurs polychromes.

PORCELAINES DE SAXE

91 — Deux jolis petits vases, forme dite pot pourri, à couvercle en ancienne porcelaine de Saxe, à festons de fleurs polychrômes et rosaces sur fond jaune haut et bas.

92 — Garniture de trois petits vases en ancienne porcelaine de Saxe dont un de forme oblongue à festons de laurier en relief et rosaces gaufrées rehaussées d'or, et les deux autres en forme de balustre à deux anses à gorge à imbrications vertes et festons de laurier en relief et rehaussés d'or.

93 — Plateau forme feuille à trois places en vieux Saxe décoré de fleurs.

94 — Saucière oblongue à deux anses et à quatre pieds en ancienne porcelaine de Saxe à bords gaufrés et décorée de fleurs peintes.

PORCELAINES DE CHINE

95 — Grande vasque en ancienne porcelaine de Chine, décorée en émaux de la famille rose à fleurs, oiseaux et ornements.

96 — Chimère assise, en porcelaine jaspée rouge et violet de la Chine, sur pied en bois de fer.

97 — Deux vases en forme de balustre en porcelaine de Chine émaillée rouge haricot.

98 — Bol en porcelaine de Chine, décoré de fleurs arabesques émaillées en couleurs.

99 — Quatre très petits bols en porcelaine de Chine, très finement décorés de divinités et d'ornements émaillés.

100 — Deux grandes chimères chinoises en terre émaillée.

101-102 — Deux paires de potiches en ancienne porcelaine de Chine, décorées en émaux de la famille verte.

BRONZES D'AMEUBLEMENT

103 — Grande et belle paire de candélabres du temps de Louis XVI, modèle à trépied à têtes d'aigles en bronze doré et vase argenté d'où s'échappent dix branches à rinceaux porte-lumières en bronze doré. La branche centrale se termine par un cornet garni de branches de vigne.

104 — Deux candélabres composés des figures de Vénus et de Mercure en bronze vert, tenant chacun un groupe de trois branches porte-lumières en bronze ciselé et doré. Sur socles Louis XVI en albâtre oriental et bronze doré.

105 — Pendule du temps de Louis XVI, en bronze doré au mat et marbre blanc à figures de nymphe et d'amour.

106 — Paire de grands et beaux bras du temps de Louis XVI, en bronze doré à l'or moulu, formés chacun d'un flambeau d'où s'échappent trois branches porte-lumières à rinceaux.

107 — Deux autres bras Louis XVI à trois lumières en bronze doré, ornés de mufles de lion et surmontés de vases garnis de festons de lauriers.

108 — Deux cadres en bronze doré à moulures ornées et écussons rapportés dans les angles.

109 — Joli lustre ancien en cuivre et cristaux de roche à neuf lumières. Quelques pièces de la partie supérieure de la colonne sont en verre de Bohême.

110 — Deux grandes appliques à trois lumières en bronze doré, composées d'ornements de style rocaille.

111 — Deux candélabres en bronze doré, formés de vases ovoïdes à deux anses et garnis de bouquets de tulipes à quatre lumières. Époque Louis XVI.

MEUBLES

112 — Miroir métallique de forme rectangulaire, dans un cadre en bois sculpté à pilastres et ornements et rehaussé de dorure. La plaque destinée à dissimuler le miroir est décorée de dragons ailés et d'ornements. XVIe siècle.

113 — Devant de bahut composé de deux jolis panneaux rectangulaires en bois de noyer sculpté en bas-relief et représentant des sujets tirés de l'histoire romaine encadrés d'ornements et d'enroulements. XVIe siècle.

114 — Joli fronton en bois sculpté à mascarons et feuillages. XVIe siècle.

115 — Joli meuble à deux corps et à fronton découpé, en bois de noyer sculpté à figures et ornements et enrichi d'incrustations de marbre. XVIe siècle.

116 — Gaine Louis XVI en bois sculpté et peint à l'imitation du marbre, avec ornements sculptés et bronzés.

117 — Commode forme demi-ronde en bois de rose et bois violet, garnie de cuivres et à dessus de marbre.

117 *bis* — Console en bois sculpté et doré à dessus de marbre.

118 — Cheminée démontée en marbre gris, avec frise en marbre blanc sculpté à jeux d'enfants.

119 — Console Louis XVI à bouts arrondis en bois d'acajou, garnie de bronzes ciselés et dorés. Dessus de marbre blanc et tablette d'entre-jambes en acajou.

120 — Beau meuble à deux corps en bois de fer sculpté à figures, ornements et dragons. La partie inférieure ferme à deux portes et le haut formant étagère est surmonté d'un pavillon orné. Beau travail chinois.

121 — Grand meuble flamand en bois noir sculpté fermant à deux portes et orné de demi-colonnes. Ses ferrures sont gravées. XVIIe siècle.

122 — Deux supports ou tables rondes à quatre pieds en bois de fer sculpté et découpé à jour, avec tablette de marbre sur le dessus.

123 — Deux sièges à X en bois sculpté, couverts en peluche ponceau et broderies au point de Hongrie.

ÉTOFFES & TAPISSERIES

124 — Tapis portière en soie bleue, richement brodé à fleurs et oiseau en soie jaune d'or et garni d'une frange. XVIIe siècle.

125 — Belle coupe de frange bleue très haute et à grille rehaussée de parties métalliques. Travail ancien.

126 — Lot de passementerie moderne : embrasses, galons, etc.

RED. :

16

0 1 2 3 4 5 6 7 8 9 10

www.ingramcontent.com/pod-product-compliance
Ingram Content Group UK Ltd.
Pitfield, Milton Keynes, MK11 3LW, UK
UKHW021036180726
13838UKWH00004B/1843

9 782329 329802